L.A. HUSTLE

L.A. HUSTLE

A DIGGER SHARMA MYSTERY

BILLIE TRAGER

L.A. Hustle

© 2023 by Billie Trager

Editors: Josh Owens, Deborah Froese
Cover and Interior Design: Emma Elzinga

Indigo River Publishing
3 West Garden Street, Ste. 718
Pensacola, FL 32502
www.indigoriverpublishing.com

Ordering Information:
Quantity Sales: Special discounts are available on quantity purchases by corporations, associations, and others. For details, contact the publisher at the address above.
Orders by US trade bookstores and wholesalers: Please contact the publisher at the address above.

Printed in the United States of America

Library of Congress Control Number: 2022919356
ISBN: 978-1-954676-42-8 (paperback) 978-1-954676-43-5 (ebook)

First Edition

With Indigo River Publishing, you can always expect great books, strong voices, and meaningful messages. Most importantly, you'll always find . . . *words worth reading.*

In loving memory of
Stuart Krassner
and
Bob Thomas

"L.A. is like paradise with a lobotomy."

– NEIL SIMON

CHAPTER 1

THE PLACE IN Stone Canyon loomed larger than I had expected. I checked the address on a piece of paper: 30279 Beverly Glen Road. Yup, the right house. The number I'd scribbled down matched the number written in some fancy script a foot high on a wooden sign adorned with roses. Ugh. I hate the rich. But they frequently pay my bills.

Undulating lawns straight out of a magazine concealed a Tudor-style mansion nestled behind a leafy copse of elm trees only a few hundred yards from the Upper Reservoir. A few hundred yards and a thousand miles. The intoxicating scent of sage drifted around me. This part of L.A. always smells of sage or junipers. You could almost see the hills through the smog, so you knew you were in the ritzy part of town. Birds twittered in the hedges—robins, finches, and sparrows. The sound soothed me.

The house was larger than its neighbors by plenty. Not out of place, mind you, here in the nice part of town. On the other hand, my sensible if classic maroon sedan glinting under the afternoon sun in the long, arc-shaped driveway seemed way out of place. I couldn't bear to part with the 1970s relic even though many enticing new models had come and gone in the ensuing twenty-some years.

When I rang the doorbell, a tight-faced woman in a tight black suit answered and guided me into a room where my dusky appearance seemed even more out of place than my car in the driveway.

She looked down her nose as if to say, *try not to touch anything.* "Sit," she ordered, pointing to the sofa.

I sat. Then, just for laughs, I barked out loud, "I can roll over and play dead too." I smiled my most winning smile.

She gave me another look that seemed to say *I wouldn't care if you got run over by a cement mixer.* Then she smiled and left looking just like the nasty neighbor in *The Wizard of Oz.* Miss Gulch.

Brrrr. Gives me the shivers just to think of that smile. You coulda chilled champagne in it. So I sat and waited. I half expected Miss Gulch to bring me a dog biscuit but instead she returned with the lady of the house—as Gulch called her—the lady who had sounded like Lauren Bacall on the telephone. Husky and arrogant.

Carmen Sloan. The last name rang a bell but I didn't know why. I stood up to shake hands with her.

She didn't look anything like Bacall. Didn't have the effortless style or sultry appeal. She looked good, but the kind of good that takes a long time to get right, from the mauve eye shadow to the slight upturn at the corners of her lips. Still, good's good, and she looked *really* good.

She turned to Miss Gulch. "Thank you, Frida."

Ms. Gulch sniffed and turned to leave, but not before looking me up and down, from my partially unbuttoned shirt to my penniless penny loafers. I'm pretty sure she was thinking that she would have to fumigate after I left.

"Mr. Sharma. Thanks for coming at such short notice," Mrs. Sloan said.

"No problem."

We studied each other for a moment. "You're not as tall as I expected," she observed.

I laughed. She and I were about the same height. "Did I sound tall on the phone?"

"No. It's just that somehow I always picture Indian men as tall."

"Depends on their parents."

"What about yours?"

"My parents?"

"Yes."

"Neither were particularly tall. My mother's Irish, my father originally from India. But I grew up in the States. I've never even been to India."

"That explains your green eyes."

"And my passion for Riverdance."

She frowned, clearly not amused. "And your name. What does the *D* stand for?"

"Digger."

"Oh."

I figured it wouldn't be long before she lit a cigarette. Sure enough, after another moment of studying me, she took a drag, eyed me slantwise, and blew out the smoke in a way that I thought was supposed to impress me. "I guess I also expect detectives to be tall, like in the movies."

"Sorry to disappoint," I said.

"Well, as long as you can do what I hired you to do, I don't care if you're an autosomal-dominant genetic dwarf."

Wow. Hadn't expected the fancy vocab. "What do you want me to do?"

She studied me some more. Then she turned her back, taking a long drag on her cigarette, and looked toward the window where birds fluttered in the hedgerow. You couldn't hear the twittering inside the house with the front windows closed. Too well insulated. The back windows were open though, a fresh breeze wafting through.

She squashed out her cigarette and after a moment, lit another.

Hard to read this one.

"How do I know I can trust you?" she asked. Her voiced quavered. It's not easy to be Bacall, even if you're a chain smoker.

I eyed her levelly. "If you trusted Bernie, you can trust me. Don't you trust Bernie?" I worked with Bernie sometimes. LAPD. I couldn't imagine how he knew her.

"I didn't say that," she snapped. "It's just . . ." Her voice cracked. She bit her lip. Pretty soon, I figured, the waterworks. Again, she didn't disappoint. I waited an awkward moment while dew drops meandered down her cheeks. She straightened and wiped away her tears pretty quick, though. Impressive.

She turned to a sideboard where a silver platter with several lead crystal glasses and a few decanters stood at attention but a bit lost and forlorn, like chess pieces removed from the board.

I wondered how often she visited them.

She poured herself a drink with some ice and turned to me.

"Drink?"

I shook my head. "I'll take some water."

"Ice?"

"No, I take mine neat."

Without smiling, she passed me a glass and sat down, staring straight ahead, looking lost. I remained standing. Then she turned her gaze to me. "My husband's having an affair." The chill in her voice would have impressed a polar bear, even a cynical one.

I waited, ever the cynical polar bear.

"At least I'm pretty sure of it," she continued. She didn't sound sure. Or at least, like she didn't want to be sure.

I waited some more. I find it's better sometimes to say nothing. It unnerves people and they occasionally reveal truths they hadn't intended to.

"I don't think it's jealousy. I . . . I've found receipts for hotel rooms, dresses, jewelry, stuff like that." She seemed to be warming up now. "And sometimes the phone rings but there's no one there . . ."

"Go on," I coaxed.

She looked away, drawing smoke into her lungs with less pretense, more like the desperate drags of the nicotine addict. "I want to hire you to help me."

"Help you what?"

"I want a divorce. I need someone to get evidence for me so I can get a decent settlement."

"Sounds like you've got evidence. Why don't you just get a lawyer?"

"I haven't . . . that is, I don't think what I've got now is enough to go on. Besides, my husband's a lawyer, and he knows everybody in town."

Ah. I knew I recognized Carmen's last name. A recent case in the papers, a civil rights case with a lawyer named Sloan. I could look it up later. "Then hire someone from out of town."

"I can't do that."

"Can't? Or don't want to?"

"All right. Don't want to."

"Well, he must have enemies. All good lawyers have enemies. Find some-one he screwed over. I'm sure they'd jump at the chance to get even."

"I don't want to do that either. The thing is, I don't want anyone to know about this until I have more proof."

I had to laugh.

"Don't laugh at me!" she flashed.

"I'm not laughing at you," I said softly. "It sounds more like you're not sure if he's being unfaithful and want me to find out."

She looked away. "Yes. Something like that." She stood up and paced for a moment before flopping on the settee. While she lit another cigarette, I looked around at the place. Nice, I guess, if you like that kind of stuff. Proba-bly decorated by a fancy-name designer who had charged a fancy price so that Sloan's friends could admire his tastefully designed living room along with his tastefully designed wife.

A high-beamed ceiling canopied a collection of mission-style furniture squatting on carpets with jagged, Southwestern Native American patterns. Equally Southwestern and Native American paintings hung on the walls. Musta come with a fancy price. The faint scent of oranges drifted through an enormous bay window that opened onto a large yard with a swimming pool and a garden. Trees rimmed the edge of the property, blocking off any view of the canyon behind. A wall of privacy.

To keep people out, or in?

I tugged my collar and imagined sitting in the shade of the trees. Far off, the air conditioning rumbled.

The only thing that seemed remotely out of place was a large oil painting above the mantelpiece. I walked over to look at it, keeping an eye on her as I did so. She kept her eyes on me too, watching my every move, her cheeks flushed.

The painting itself seemed too amateurish to be hanging in this room. Clearly executed by someone who had studied Cubism. Someone who had studied but not mastered it. The picture featured the fractured, multiple per-

spectives and geometric forms so common to the school but they lacked the
simplicity or elegance seen in Picasso's works. Well done, but not great. From
what I could tell, the subject was a nude woman, fragments of her body separated and embedded in various elements of modern life such as bedrooms, ca-
fes, cars, buildings, traffic lights, and so forth. It had the charm so common to
amateur paintings but still clashed with the rest of the furnishings. Curious,
I searched the lower-right corner for a signature and to my surprise, saw the
name *Carmen* painted there in a style reminiscent of Picasso's own signature.

I turned back to study Carmen Sloan and she looked away. I'd pegged
her as a trophy wife, but maybe I hadn't done her justice. She didn't wear a
wedding ring. The painting on the wall reflected aspects of her that were not
readily apparent on my first superficial examination. True, she had that kind
of "pretty" that trophy wives have, but beneath that, *hmmm!* Mocha skin and
large, dark eyes, wide set like Britney Spears. Her hair started out black and
faded to blonde.

Two feelings about her wrestled with each other: an attraction and urge
to rescue her. That meant trouble. And plenty of it.

In a former life, I'd learned the hard way that when a gal started making
me feel like rescuing her, it usually meant that she had some tough problems
that would soon become my problems. I looked at the picture again. A trou-
bled hand had painted it. I thought about asking Carmen what it meant but
realized that would be falling back into old habits. Somewhat bitter, I decided
to change tack and play the wise father confessor. "Mrs. Sloan?"

"Call me Carmen."

"No."

"Okay."

"I think I've got a pretty good idea what's going on here. You're what,
thirty?"

She nodded.

"And your husband, he's, what, forty?"

"Thirty-eight."

"You married him young. Maybe you wanted to get out of the house? He
made you promises no one had made before. He could give you things you

had always wanted."

She nodded again.

"He made you sign a prenup, right?"

"How did you know?" Her eyebrows shot up and her eyes widened.

"I've been doing this for a while Mrs. Sloan."

"Call me Carmen."

"No."

She sank back on the settee, somewhat deflated.

"So you married him and he gave you everything you wanted, but he wasn't there for you emotionally. And then you realized he wasn't such a nice guy, that he had become bored with you, and that you had become just another ornament in his ornamental life."

Sullen and glazed, she nodded dully as I continued. "Sure, he gave you everything you wanted, gave you plenty of money, but that's never enough. He spent less and less time at home, showed less interest in being with you, started going on more business trips. Then you started noticing suspicious things."

She fumbled with her gold-plated cigarette case but said nothing.

Now for the zinger. "What part of the OC are you from?" I asked.

She started, almost dropping the case, but then she set it down on the coffee tablet, flushing. "How did you know that?"

"Lucky guess."

Actually not. It's just that good-looking girls from not-as-ritzy-as-Newport Beach towns in Orange County always marry well-heeled lawyers from Beverly Hills. They think the high life will fill the void. It never does. They think their husbands will be faithful. They never are. They become depressed. Then they call me.

I could have told her all that, but it would have just made her feel bad. Even before she said it, I knew she would answer my question with something like Santa Ana, Costa Mesa, or Seal Beach, or from one of the good—

"—one of the good parts of Huntington Beach," she said.

"Nice town."

"Yeah, sure, I guess. I couldn't wait to leave."

"That why you married him?"

She didn't answer, the pain on her face eloquent enough. She lighted another cigarette, stood, and walked to the front windows. Two robins fought over something on the lawn. A scrap of food. A female. Territory. Who knew? She watched them for a moment before turning back to stare at me, saying nothing, her expression inscrutable.

"Look, Mrs. Sloan," I said. "I'll take the case. I can help you. If you want references, here are a couple that should ease your mind about trusting me." I handed her a card.

She perused the card then looked up at me, hope in her eyes.

"I'll take your case, but on one condition."

"What's that?"

"I'm gonna watch your husband to see if he's cheating on you. If he is, I'll get proof. If he's not, at least you'll know. And that's all I'm gonna do."

"That's all I want."

"Is it?"

"What are you saying?"

"It's happened before that when a gal says she wants me to help her get a divorce what she really wants is for me to get her life straight for her."

She flushed. "I don't know what you mean."

I smiled inwardly. She probably didn't. It didn't make any difference. I knew I was right. "Anyway, I'll need a picture of your husband—what's his first name, by the way?"

"Lamont."

"Okay. And his work address and number would be helpful."

She fetched a silver case from the sideboard and handed me one of his cards. Nothing remarkable about it: *Lamont Sloan, Attorney at Law, Wilshire Boulevard.*

I could picture him now with his slicked-back hair, cruising along in a silver current-model Black Forest sports car complete with leather accessories and tinted windows. I hated him already. "My retainer's two grand. I charge five hundred a day plus expenses. Also, a copy of your phone bill and those receipts you were telling me about would be useful."

Without hesitation, she fetched a Louis Vuitton purse from one of the end tables, opened her wallet, and handed me twenty one-hundred-dollar bills as if they were Monopoly money, counting them out with the precision of a bank teller. It never ceases to amaze me how free people are with other people's cash.

She then dug a manila folder from the purse and handed it to me silently. I glanced inside to find photocopies of bills, receipts, and so on. Well prepared. I looked up to thank her and she twirled away, stirring her perfume in the air.

Subtle. Very subtle. She impressed me again. Twice in one day. Not bad.

CHAPTER 2

TRAFFIC SUCKED. A noisy, angry stream of people who hated each other simply for existing moving in jerking fits and stops. They don't understand why and they don't care. They just want to get home or to work or somewhere—anywhere. Most of 'em can't even see the cities they live in, their houses, or their apartments, through the dirty haze. I hate L.A. Jack Kerouac once called it the loneliest and most brutal city in America.

Los Angeles. The City of Angels, a beauty parlor at the end of the universe, paradise with a lobotomy, a bright and glitzy place. Today's weather forecast: smoggy.

The silver lining, my first micromance of the day. You know what a micromance is, right? When you see an attractive person somewhere and you don't get the chance to spend more than a few seconds admiring them. They make eye contact and seem to find you attractive as well. But then you both go about your day and you realize you'll never see each other again. It happens when two people lock gazes from different trains moving apart, pass on the street, or—most commonly in L.A.—peer voyeuristically into one another's cars.

In this case, my micromance involved two stunning Asians in a canary yellow Porsche coupe stopped briefly in the stalled traffic. Neither looked older than twenty, but the car, idling with a hypnotic thrum, looked to cost plenty. They both had straight coal-black hair, one cut in a short bob, the other wearing it well below her shoulders. They met my gaze and I smiled. They rewarded me with two dazzling smiles in return.

Then the one in the passenger seat rolled down her window. I rolled down mine.

"Hey cutie!" she chirped in an accent I couldn't place.

"Hey gorgeous!" I chirruped back.

"Where you headed?"

"On my way to work. You?"

"We're going clubbing!"

"At one in the afternoon?"

"We know where to go!"

"Nice!"

"You wanna go with us?" she teased.

Although sorely tempted, they were way too young for me. "Sorry," I replied, "but I got a girlfriend and I gotta get to work."

"Oh, that's too bad," she pouted. Then she reached down somewhere down by her feet and produced a rose. She handed it across to me. "To remember us!" She flashed another winning smile.

"Oh, I couldn't forget you two," I flirted back.

"Bye now!" she drawled, rolling up the window.

Ignoring the honking behind me, I changed lanes to get off at my exit and felt a micropang of sadness. I rolled up my window, inhaling the heady scent of the rose. I set it down carefully on the passenger seat, pricking my finger. I sucked at the cut, tasting blood, vaguely disappointed in myself, wondering if I should have joined them after all. My finger throbbed. *Well, that's love for you,* I thought.

The day burned hotter than I had expected, and a blanket of heat had steamed in through the open window. The AC soon cooled me back down, but I could tell we were in for an inferno. The kind of day that makes women swoon and men kill each other. I didn't plan on getting killed or killing anyone though, and I'd already made the cute Asian girls swoon, so I guided the sensible maroon sedan—hereafter, SMS—back to Old Town Pasadena and descended to the subterranean garage that lay like a mournful afterthought beneath my Mediterranean apartment complex. Cool and quiet here.

As I rode the elevator to the third floor, yawning and assessing myself in the mirrored wall, my mobile phone vibrated against my right hip. "Hello, Josh" I said, frantically fumbling for the volume. Caller ID's a wonderful thing.

Josh bellowed my name before I could adjust the sound level, so I held the phone away from my ear until I could turn it down. "I know you're across town, Josh, but we're using this wonderful invention, the telephone. No need to shout. I can hear you just fine."

"Sorry Digger, it's just that I've got something here I didn't want to sit on."

"What? A Whoopee Cushion?"

"Ha ha!" he roared again. "No, something that might interest you."

"Oh?"

"Yeah. How soon can you get down here?"

"Oh, I dunno." I checked my watch. "If I leave before three, I should miss the traffic." Untrue, of course. There's always traffic. "How about fourish?"

"Great!"

I moved the phone a few inches away from my ear. "See you."

My apartment. My oasis. Cool and dark. I turned on a lamp but didn't open the shades to the balcony. Maybe later. The mail contained the usual things you see in a bachelor's post: offers to refinance my house (which I no longer owned); offers for free samples of medication (Viagra, which I definitely didn't need); the latest Franklin Library selection (*Cry the Beloved Country,* by Alan Paton); credit cards ("unlimited miles!"); and, of course, a letter from my attorney, asking for monthly payment.

An old friend named Singleton Webb had sent a post-card from Crete, an island off the coast of Greece. Quite beautiful. I needed more tropical vacations. For a moment, I hated him for having gone to such a nice place.

I peered inside the fridge only to find the usual thing you see in a bachelor's fridge: film. I turned on my excellent stereo, the sole remnant of a former life. Renée Fleming's sultry voice coiled through the apartment like smoke. Very soothing. I thought about Carmen Sloan's perfume. Then I thought about her legs. Then I thought, *I'm thinking a little too much about a client in the wrong way.*

She needed help, that's for sure. She didn't need a private detective; she needed a shrink. Still, when a problem has legs like that, a guy could use a drink. I got a glass of ginger ale and bitters and cursed my genetic inability to stomach booze like the tough detectives in books.

I then ruminated on my genes. My father. Sometimes I wondered what kind of guy he had been. I'd never met him. He'd never tried to contact me so I returned the favor. My mother, an Irish beauty of a bygone era, had fallen for him when they were both at UC Berkeley.

He vanished like one of his ancestral swamis when he found out he had, well, you know, I guess, knocked her up. Only I don't like to think about my mother that way. She said she never knew where he went. Maybe. Either way, all she got was a "Dear Molly" letter and all I got was semi-dark skin and hunter-green eyes that had been described as everything from "haunting" to "haunted" to "the masked trap door to that vile darkness of your infernal soul."

The latter made me give up dating English majors in college. I don't mind being criticized as long as I understand the words.

The answering machine blinked insistently, so I pressed the "play" button to humor it. A message from my attorney's secretary, reminding me pleasantly about my monthly payment, "in case you didn't get our correspondence." Subtle as a flying hatchet, my lawyer, and with all the unctuous charm of a used condom. But a good attorney. Well, maybe not that good. I still paid alimony. A message from the apartment manager about a termite inspection. One from my dear mother, asking me to call her back right away because she had something very important to tell me. I groaned. No way could I talk to Mom right now. I flopped down on the couch and nursed my drink, trying to feel like the tough guy I clearly wasn't.

After a few minutes of idleness, I jumped into the shower to wash off several layers of Los Angeles and put on fresh clothes. I dressed lighter and more casually this time but still nice. After all, I was going to see one of L.A.'s finest. But not fine enough to warrant a dress shirt.

I nosed the SMS down the 110, traffic moving pretty good until I hit the 5, a lousy, crummy, steaming cesspool of a parking lot. Fortunately, with the windows up and the AC on, I couldn't hear the rumble of the cars around me. I turned on the radio and the cheery if dulcet tones of Jim Ladd, DJ on KLOS—"We lost our minds for a moment but we're okay now!"—wafted through the speakers. "And now an oldie but goodie from 1982 by Prince! A song whose time has finally come. You know they'll be shouting this one from the rooftops on New Year's Eve!"

As the thundering drums and syrupy synths of Prince's catchy song pounded hypnotically into my brain, I glanced around, hoping to catch the eye of a cute girl and maybe even be rewarded with a smile. But everyone else looked either as bored as I felt or inanimate. Clearly the freeway was not the way to go today. I knew a few surface street shortcuts, so I pulled off. Fifteen minutes later, I parked in the visitor's lot of the LAPD substation on San Pedro Avenue. A few minutes after that, I sat enjoying the cool half-darkness of Josh's office, my salmon pink golfing shirt sticking to me like a second skin.

Josh was an angular man with irregular angles. His iron-spiked hair shot off in more directions than a drunken pastor's sermon, and none of his limbs looked like they had formed as part of a matched set. His piercing French blue eyes bore through me, making me feel vaguely guilty. His smile could charm snakes.

This outside awkwardness couldn't have been a more deceptive reflection of the inner man, one of the most generous people I knew. I trusted him completely. Well, as much as I trust anyone.

Not a helluva lot.

"Digger! You look like hell," Josh boomed, his voice as loud in person as on the phone.

"Thanks. I fractured my left nipple in a freak yogurt-eating contest accident."

"I don't even know what that means," he laughed.

"Never mind. You look like you got up early this morning to fight the forces of evil threatening the law-abiding denizens of our fair city," I scoffed.

He rolled his eyes. "Always the wise guy. Anyway, I've got something for you," he said. "S'right up your alley."

"Oh?"

"Yeah. You remember Eddie Blake, who used to be in homicide?" He watched me closely, his gaze not wavering.

"The short guy with the limp?" I countered, watching him just as closely.

"That's the one. Anyway, he got out of the service and went private, like you."

"Okay. What about him?" I asked.

"Well, it seems he kind of specializes, and he doesn't handle everything that comes his way. We were talking the other day and he asked me if I knew anyone who might be interested in a case not in his line. I thought of you, but figured I should ask before I told him *yes* or *no*. So I just told him I'd get back to him. He told me a little about the case. If you're interested."

"*Hmmm*. I'm already working on a case now."

"Really?" He stared even more intently.

"Yeah."

He cocked his head and spread his hands as if to ask, *what about?*

"Sorry. Boring, private, matrimonial work."

He raised his eyebrows. "I thought you'd given up that kind of work. I mean, after, um . . ." he trailed off awkwardly.

I picked up a paper clip off his desk and unbent it.

"Yeah, I had, but . . ."

He waited.

"But, I dunno, there was something about this case," I concluded, lamely.

"Something with a firm ass and a nice rack, I'll bet!" he laughed. "Digger, you son-of-a-bitch!" He shook his head. "You'll never learn, will you?"

"Actually, there's a nice backside in the picture, but I'm more interested in her husband."

He shook his head again, "Yeah, yeah. I know, but really . . . isn't there something in your personal code that says you never screw your clients?"

"First of all, he's not my client, she is. And secondly, I'm not gonna screw her. But yes, that's my code of ethics, such as it is."

"*Ahhh*." Josh watched me mangle another of his paperclips. "Sorry. Didn't mean to . . . you know."

"Don't worry about it. Good to hear it unsanitized." The words came out more sarcastically than I intended them.

He smiled. "Okay."

"Anyway, I usually work on only one case at a time."

"I know, I know. Well, lemme tell you about it, then you can decide."

"Okay. I'm game."

He poured himself a cola and poured me a glass of ginger ale. He didn't have any bitters. Still, it's always nice when your friends remember your short-comings and preferences. In fact, I think we usually like people because we can tolerate their faults rather than because of their good points.

After handing me my drink, he sat down and sipped his cola for a moment. "What do you know about finding lost people?"

"Depends upon how lost they are and how much I want to find them."

He smiled. "And how much they want to be found."

I nodded.

"This case did go through missing persons, but they came up with nada. The guy's name is, uh, um . . ." He flipped through some notes on his desk, pulling out a slip of paper. "Noakes, Alfie Noakes. N-O-A-K-E-S. Anyway, somebody approached Blake on the outside wanting to find this Noakes, and Blake told them he would think about it."

"Who?"

"I dunno. I didn't ask."

"Why not?"

"I dunno. I just got this feeling he didn't want me to." He shrugged.

"*Hmmm*. What about missing persons. Who reported him lost?"

"Sorry, Digger. I don't know that either."

"Just a wealth of information, aren't you?"

Josh laughed and leaned back in his chair, downing more of his cola. "Well, I may not know much, but I do know that they promised to pay well."

I cocked my head.

"A little extra goes a long way, huh, Digger?"

I had to smile. "How did you know that I was, well, a little hard up?"

He tried to look sly, which was impossible with his bushy eyebrows and fleshy jowls. Instead, he ended up looking constipated. "We have our ways of knowing, Digger. We have our ways. And when I hear a friend's down and out, I like to help."

I couldn't dispute that. I mean, I wasn't behind on the rent or anything, but my standard of living had dipped below what I would have liked. I thought about it a bit more and figured I could always check out this missing person case and start on it when I was done with Carmen Sloan. I mean, Carmen Sloan's *case*. Of course, that's what I mean. Right. Anyway, that wouldn't take more than a week or so, and it didn't seem like the lost man would get any more lost.

It couldn't hurt to check it out.

"All right," I said. "What's Blake's number?"

CHAPTER 3

LATER THAT EVENING, I pulled up in front of a small stucco, Spanish-style home in the Bungalow Heaven neighborhood to pick up my girlfriend, Belle. I liked her place. It was nestled between two much larger houses like someone's kid brother but much more elegant than the MacMansions looming on either side. Bungalow Heaven was starting to become as much of a myth as the more famous one.

Actually, *girlfriend* might not be an accurate term. Mine, not hers. Crazy about her, even though she could be a nuisance at times. She liked me too but had steadfastly resisted becoming exclusive, saying she liked her freedom. I knew she saw other guys but it didn't matter to me, and I didn't see other women. Not my style. I had showered—again—and dressed up rather smartly in khakis and a sky-blue, button-down shirt. No tie though. I hate ties. She had a cat called Schrodinger, but I had never seen it and didn't even know if it existed.

An adorable little blonde opened the door the instant I pressed the bell, and before I could react, she threw her arms around my neck and kissed me. I kissed back.

"Digger!"

"Belle!"

She eyed me thoughtfully. "What have you been around to today?"

"Nothing. Why?" I suppressed a smile at her odd word choice.

"Hmm." She tilted her head to one side and squinted at me. "You're on top of a case, aren't you?"

I laughed as much out of surprise as at her unusual phrasing. "How did you know?"

"You've got that faraway look in your eyes that you get when you're on top of a case."

Well, on top of two cases, but I admired her powers of deduction. "Yes, you're right. You're very clever. I'm on top of a case. Can we go eat? I'm starved."

"Ha ha! Yeah, right. Okay. Gimme a minute."

I made to follow her into the house but as soon as I stepped over the threshold, she stopped me with a hand on my chest. She kissed me again. "You can't come in. I'm on my cycle."

"That's just as well. You know the sight of blood makes me queasy."

She laughed.

I searched for a compliment. "Your skin looks radiant!"

"I just exfoliated."

"Oh," I said, deflated.

She laughed again. "Back in a minute!"

I watched her trip lightly down the hallway and disappear into her bedroom, doing god knows what. One of those subtle things that women have to do before they leave the house but that remains a mystery to men. In my experience, it's best not to try to figure out what they're up to. You wouldn't understand it anyway. I peered around in the dim light looking for Schrodinger, but as usual, he was nowhere to be found.

She bounced back from the bedroom and my heart sped up a bit. Cute but annoying. She came from some wealthy family in Spain, or more precisely, Barcelona. A word to the wise: Catalonians do *not* consider themselves Spanish. I made that mistaken assumption. Once. Anyway, she had come to the US as a young woman to study at Yale and eventually wound up on the faculty at UCLA as a professor of chemistry. I liked to think she and I had good chemistry but it might have been just her. She had a very sweet accent that most people were unable to place because she had lived in the States for so long and spoke excellent English—apart from some quirks. She had only a few flaws. One, she was very talkative, which I don't like. The other, she was a kleptomaniac, which for some reason didn't bother me much. Go figure.

She wore a beautiful dress the color of wet flowerpots with a white, flowing, see-through scarf and open-toed sandals. She looked stunning. Suddenly, I found myself rethinking my choice of evening dress. I shoulda upped my game. I worried about the SMS as well, wondering if all that gorgeousness might melt into a droopy puddle at the sight of it. Maybe one of these days I should get myself a cool convertible. But the SMS and I had been through a lot together. Anyway, we weren't going anywhere fancy. I opened the passenger side door for her. She liked my Old-World charm.

As I said before, she could be annoying but only because she talked incessantly. As we drove to the restaurant through the early evening traffic—bad, but not as bad as rush hour—she told me about some recent discovery in molecular biology. Even though only half-listening, entranced by her perfume, I caught most of what she said. I also noticed out of the corner of my eye she had palmed my Chapstick and eased it into her purse.

"I thought you were a chemist. Why this sudden interest in molecular biology?" I inquired.

"Oh, *novio*!" she said, punching me lightly on the shoulder. "You know that as an undergraduate I examined biology!"

"Of course," I slapped my forehead. "How could I forget?"

She laughed and took my hand. "You're so cute!"

I kissed her hand.

A few minutes later, we pulled up at one of our favorite joints, Casablanca, a Moroccan restaurant.

Even though I had made reservations, we waited for a table in the packed and noisy entrance. In the dimly lit, hazy interior, ghostly shapes in the form of servers and belly dancers flitted before my eyes. From hidden speakers, the seductive tones of the oud, kamenjah, and qanun, swirled around us. My mouth started watering as the scent of cinnamon, cumin, turmeric, ginger, paprika, cloves, fennel, and nutmeg enveloped us. Belle put her arm around me and warmed me up even more by nestling her face into my neck and kissing it.

She periodically grabbed soft mints from a glass bowl and stuffed them in my mouth, knowing that I can get hangry.

Eventually, a diminutive server—after glaring pointedly to the empty mint dish—led us to a table near the kitchen. Still noisy, but at least we could hear each other.

"So *novio*, are you going to tell me about this case?" Belle asked.

"Why do you want to know?"

We sipped at sweet drinks of some unknown variety.

"Well, if it's a cute guy, I'll be interested in meeting him," she teased.

"Okay."

"And if it's a pretty girl, I'll be jealous."

"You never get jealous!"

"That's beside the point."

She smiled her beautiful smile as she slipped a fork from her set of silverware. It disappeared beneath the table.

"Okay, honey. If you think you can contain your insane jealousy." I told her about my encounter with Carmen Sloan but not my meeting with Josh. I figured one case was all she could handle at this point. Hell, it was all I could handle.

She tapped her teeth with her fingernail, her habit when thinking. Finally, she nodded. "That woman's lying to you."

"Lying? How do you know?"

"*Novio*, a woman knows when her man's cheating on her. She doesn't hire someone like you to find out for her."

"Then why hire me?"

"I don't know. Did she see a picture of you before you met? That would explain it."

"Ha ha. No, she didn't. Not that I know of."

"And a lot of the other things she told you were lies too."

"Oh, really? Like what?"

"That she doesn't know any lawyers to hire. Lawyers' wives mingle only with other lawyers' wives. It's a completed circle."

"A completed circle, eh?"

"Yes. That woman's dangerous and she's not telling you the truth. Not any of it."

"I see." I pondered this. "But I can't just confront her."

"Oh, you won't have to. Eventually what she really wants will come out. How did she find out about you?"

"A lawyer friend of mine named Bernie."

"Oh, okay."

"Why?"

"Just . . . oh, nothing."

I shrugged.

"Be careful with this woman, *novio*. She sounds devious." She pronounced the last word as if it had about ten syllables.

"Okay. I promise."

We were interrupted by one of the belly dancers who tried to pull me up to dance with her. I glanced at Belle. She just laughed and nodded. I gave in, allowing the girl to drag me out onto her dance floor.

It was wiggly and I was mortified to find my body contorting into all manner of postures it wasn't used to being in. Belle laughed the whole time.

She was still laughing when the belly dancer liberated me to return to the table and our food, which the server had brought while the belly dancer embarrassed me.

"Oh, *novio!*" Belle laughed, tears streaming down her face. "That was precious!"

I had to smile. "I wish there had been more dancing and less belly."

Later, while driving her home, she leaned against me and said, "let's go back to your place."

"I thought you were on your period?"

"That's okay."

I smiled inwardly as I turned to head home. Okay by me.

When I woke up the next morning, she had disappeared—along with my toaster.

CHAPTER 4

OVER THE NEXT several days, I did a lot of the legwork you need to do to track down a man like Lamont Sloan. I visited his offices under the pretense of being a prospective client. His perfect secretary—I couldn't help but call her Lamont's angel—apologized profusely, but Mr. Sloan couldn't possibly see me until next week.

I did a little digging and found out that he had graduated from UCLA shortly before I graduated from Cal. He went on to Hastings Law School where he graduated near the top of his class. I realized with caustic resentment that he might have even been there with me, a couple of chummy UC grads all the way.

He passed the bar his first try and then entered the firm of Waldmeyer, Michelson & Flint in San Francisco. He made associate partner in three years. He moved to L.A., opened a branch office, and a few years later made full partner. He started his own very lucrative practice about two years after that and had been at it ever since, earning money faster than he could spend it. I found him in L.A.'s *Who's Who*, but everybody's in there.

In the brief bio, it listed him as a "prominent Los Angeles attorney who made a name for himself taking on pro bono but high-profile civil rights cases—most of which he won—before going into private practice in Beverly Hills." *Hmmm.* An unexpected twist. "He lives in Los Angeles and is married to Carmen Sloan, née Gomez, of Huntington Beach. They have no children."

None that *Who's Who* knew about, anyhow.

Bitter? Naw, not me.

Couldn't find much else. Josh helped me out by looking into Sloan's criminal record. He didn't have one, but he had brought a couple of lawsuits against police officers for his clients. Mostly wrongful arrest, civil rights violations, that kind of thing. In looking through some articles I found on the L.A. Times website, a pretty clear pictured emerged that he had no friends downtown at police headquarters. Good to know.

A search of the Lexis-Nexis database retrieved plenty about Sloan, but nothing in the line of scandal. Most of the stories were about his triumphs. A spotless record as far as I could tell. Clearly, I'd have to do some more digging. Nobody in L.A. is spotless. They just hide their misdeeds well. He must have made a few enemies along the way.

I also did a little research into Carmen Sloan. Other than things I already knew about her, I discovered she had an MFA in painting from Cal State Long Beach. She steadily improved in my estimation. At first, I had pegged her as a trophy wife, probably because I deal with enough of them. But now I realized she was more complex, which only made her more interesting— that's to say, attractive. A couple of times, I thought about calling her, even going so far as to think up excuses. But that would be a bad idea.

I did call Eddie Blake a few times but couldn't get a hold of him. I left a couple messages, but he didn't call me back. The last message had been two days ago and I had mentioned Josh Cohen, hoping that might pique his interest. Still, he hadn't called. Was that any way to treat a friend of Josh Cohen? Maybe it was. Or maybe he had decided to take the case himself after all. I understood. We all gotta eat.

Or maybe he just didn't like the way I sounded on the phone or my ethnic surname. I guess it was my day to be bitter and hypersensitive.

I called Belle for consolation, but she didn't answer. I then remembered she had mentioned going to Santa Barbara for a few days with one of those pretty, pretty boys that she calls friends.

So I used the time to follow up some of the leads Carmen Sloan had given me. She got a current phone bill from the phone company and sent it to me.

Her scent lingered faintly on the paper. I spent a fruitless evening pouring over the medium lengthy list of numbers. After accounting for duplicates, I came up with about thirty or so unique numbers. Then came the task of calling all of them to see if anything turned up.

Nothing did.

Most of the numbers were easily tied to Carmen. Upscale boutiques on Rodeo Drive. No surprises there. Upscale restaurants on Santa Monica Boulevard. You know the kind of place. Places where miserable wives of rich lawyers meet to have lunch and try to convince each other how happy they are. And upscale hair salons where they charge three-hundred bucks to make you look like a French poodle. Only three numbers could be tied to Lamont Sloan and only one of those seemed remotely promising. That fizzled after I found out it was for his health club. I guessed he mostly used his mobile phone.

Of course, the list noted only outgoing calls from the house. The incoming call list might be more interesting. A list of Lamont Sloan's mobile calls might also be enlightening. It would also be just about impossible to get. For me anyway. You have to know the right people and they have to owe you favors. I couldn't think of anyone who owed me favors, let alone the right people. But Carmen Sloan could get that, right?

Right. I called her and she said she'd work on it. That left me with no leads so I followed an old-fashioned ploy that had proved useful in the past. I hauled out an old ham radio and fiddled around with it for a while until I remembered how it worked. I mounted it under the dash, which you can do only in an older car like mine. Every once in a while, driving a classic has its rewards, and I'm not talking about getting whistled at by the rough trade in Brentwood.

During the early days of the mobile craze, I found a ham radio good for more than just listening to police chatter. The older mobile phones didn't have all those built-in de-scramblers like they do now, but eventually the stoners in the Valley got bored trying to keep up with technology and eavesdropping became passé—except for those few die-hards like yours truly who did keep up with the technology. My twenty-year-old Radio Shack special worked just as good as the more sophisticated and pricey younger generation radios. Good enough for me.

As I waited at the light to turn left onto Wilshire Boulevard, I had a rather sweet micromance. A beautiful Black woman with mocha skin and cornrows in a little red Corvette convertible with the top down, waiting next to me to turn left as well. She turned to me and I smiled. She smiled back. I rolled down my driver's side window.

"Beautiful day, huh?" she asked, flashing an equally beautiful smile.

"Traffic seems heavy," I replied.

"That's not always a bad thing, is it?"

"Oh? Why?" I asked.

"We got to meet, didn't we?" She winked.

"Yeah!" I wanted to ask her for her number but the light changed and, with a quick "bye!" she made a U-turn. Again, I felt a bittersweet micropang. Don't get me wrong, I love Belle. But, you know, a guy has to have a little harmless fun now and then, right? Just because you're on a diet don't mean you can't look at the menu.

I hung out near the law offices of Lamont Sloan, Attorney at Law, conveniently located across from a coffee shop, where I studied the classifieds and drank mocha after mocha. I had already ID'd Sloan's car, a new Porsche, black, with tinted windows. Not hard to tell it was his. The plates made me love living in California: *I♥2SU4U*

After I'd gone to the bathroom for the umpteenth time, Lamont Sloan came out of his office looking very sharp in suspenders and a bow tie. It was around lunch time, so I figured he was probably going out to eat and would likely choose somewhere close by. I tailed him for a few blocks down Wilshire Boulevard before he turned left onto Fairfax Avenue. After a few more blocks, he pulled into the parking lot of a restaurant with a name I couldn't pronounce.

I drove past the restaurant, made a U-turn at the light, and drove back. I parked across the street. My little buggy would have been conspicuous in the parking lot of the eatery which I bet had more fountains than waiters and more waiters than entrees. I found out about the entrees when I dodged across the street to the sidewalk next to the restaurant. I couldn't pronounce the names of the menu items and couldn't have bought them anyway. You know how I know? No prices. If you have to ask, you can't afford it.

I strolled kind of casual-like to a newspaper dispenser in front of the restaurant, a sort of faux-bistro, with tables inside and out. I scanned the front page, figuring I was dressed well enough to do that and tried to spot Sloan. Again not hard.

He must have been hot, because he passed on the lovely outside tables for an inside booth across from the window. He had just ordered a drink and glanced at his watch. He had that look of a man waiting for someone who's running late, drumming his fingers on the table and repeatedly looking at the entrance. He downed whatever he'd ordered and called for another. He looked at his watch again and sipped his second round. I didn't know what he drank except that it wasn't clear, and it didn't have one of those little umbrellas or an olive on a toothpick shaped like a sword. He continued tapping on the table impatiently.

I didn't want to linger too long. After all, a guy like me wearing a suit like mine reads the headlines only so long before he either buys the paper or walks on.

At the light, I crossed back over to the other side of Fairfax, returned to the car, and fired up the old Radio Shack special. After fiddling with the frequency for a few minutes, a couple of mobile conversations rewarded my efforts. I didn't get Sloan. Not surprising, as he didn't have his phone out.

I listened to a young couple bickering about which private school their first grader should attend. Then a businessman begging his mistress to be discreet. A delivery boy trying to find an address. A doctor talking to his exchange. Thousands of voices hurtled through the smoggy air of L.A., like comets through the night sky. I got bored with the patter and shut off the radio.

Across the street, Sloan still sat at the same table, sipping drink after drink. After about twenty minutes, a taxi pulled up in front of the restaurant and a man wearing a dark blue double-breasted suit and a blood-red tie stepped out. He was a tall man with hawk-like features—piercing black eyes, heavy arching eyebrows and a long hooked nose. He paid the driver through the window and took a quick predatory look around. I didn't know him and didn't want to. I leaned back, out of view. When I looked again, he had gone into the restaurant and was striding toward Sloan's table. Sloan caught sight of him and stood up.

They shook hands but I could tell Sloan wasn't happy. His body language—stiff, unsmiling, furtive—betrayed a man meeting someone on their terms rather than his own. He looked angry too. But heck, from my vantage point at least a hundred feet away, maybe I mistook a man just happy to see an old buddy. I pulled out a little portable keyhole—a battered pair of binoculars which I keep for just such occasions—and put it up to my eyes. Ah, better.

The tall man sat down, ordered a drink from the waiter, and glanced at the menu, which he then snapped shut. The waiter took his and Sloan's orders, delivered by both in quick, uninterested fashion.

The two men then sat staring at each other for a few minutes. They reminded me of a couple of kids having a no-blink contest. This gave me a chance to examine the hawk-faced man more closely.

I zoomed in with my binoculars and realized that his hawkish appearance came not only from his features but also his mannerisms—a habitual jerking of his head left and right as if scanning for threats or prey with unblinking eyes. His face, crisscrossed like a tic-tac-toe board, had gotten in the way of too many sharp objects.

Finally, Sloan's lip moved. For only a sentence or two. The hawkish man nodded. Sloan said something else. The hawkish man shook his head. Sloan sat back, looking satisfied. He then fumbled in his pocket and pulled out his mobile phone.

Going on a hunch, I turned on the radio again as Sloan punched numbers into his phone. After fiddling with the frequency, I heard a smooth, cultured voice. I couldn't tell if it was Sloan until I matched his side of the conversation to the lip movements.

Not that it was much of a conversation.

The smooth voice—Sloan's—said, "Fine. That's fine."

The other voice on Sloan's phone, deep and sonorous, asked, "Did he make it all right?"

To which Sloan answered, "Yeah. He's here now. You wanna talk to him?"
"Yeah."

Sloan handed the phone to Hawkface. "Were there any problems?" Hawkface asked, his voice quiet and intense.

"No," answered Deep and Sonorous.

"Fine." A pause. "Okay, we'll meet as planned," said Hawkface.

"Okay. See you then."

The call disconnected, and Hawkface snapped the phone closed, handing it back to Sloan.

Sloan put the phone back in his pocket and reached over to slap Hawkface on the shoulder, who recoiled slightly. Sloan offered a gleaming smile, and said a few things to Hawkface, who smiled back. It was a reluctant smile, a smile from a face not used to smiling. Even from a distance, I could see the glint of gold teeth.

CHAPTER 5

AFTER TAILING SLOAN back to his office, I headed north to check out one of Carmen's receipts. I had exhausted most of them already. Several for hotels in San Francisco. Carmen told me Sloan often took business trips up there, which made sense. He had lived in the Bay Area and probably still had contacts up there. Others for retail shops that, as it turned out, everyone except me knew as "fine boutiques for ladies' clothes."

I questioned Carmen about these places.

"I'm dead certain he didn't buy me anything from them."

"Why?" I asked.

"He doesn't buy clothes for me," she snapped with an unmistakable finality.

She met my perfectly reasonable, polite inquiry, "Why do they call these places boutiques instead of stores?" with a chilly silence.

The most interesting receipt: Norman's, an upscale jeweler in Flintridge.

When I asked, Carmen told me with the same decisive tone, "My husband doesn't buy jewelry for me, either."

I actually knew about Norman's because I'd been there on a case once. The proprietor reminded me of an old movie actor called Raymond Massey; very tall, very ugly, very charming. The receipt Carmen gave me showed fifteen grand for a diamond clasp. It didn't specify more. Sloan's signature acknowledged receipt of the clasp.

I could understand Carmen's suspicions. Woman's clothing boutiques, women's jewelry, hotel rooms in other cities. An old story. The bored husband running around.

Why not? Happens all the time. Now that I'd seen him and heard his voice, it made sense. At one time, I might have been naïve enough to think that Sloan might worry about his reputation. After living in L.A. for a while, I realized that people don't have reputations anymore. They just have money.

At any rate, I'd have to check them all out.

I thought it might be a good idea to start with the jewelers since I already knew it. I assumed the man I remembered was Norman but didn't know if that was his first or last name. So I buzzed up the 2 to the 210 and then headed east past the Descanso Gardens and on into Flintridge. I had a friend once who lived in La Cañada who always called it "La Cañada/Flintridge." Oddly enough, people who live in Flintridge just call it "Flintridge." You could see the hills through the smog.

After a few lefts and rights down quiet, well-swept streets without sidewalks, I pulled the SMS into a spot a few doors past Norman's. I figured if I parked in plain view, they wouldn't talk to me. Cars mean a lot in L.A. Clothes, on the other hand, don't matter at all. The guy in the ripped tee-shirt, shorts, and sandals could be a movie mogul. My somewhat exotic appearance I could do nothing about, but there were Indian movie moguls. Granted, they were in Bollywood.

It was cool and pleasant inside. There were four large glass cases arranged at angles to one another and mirrors on the walls that made the place look huge. Even at a distance I noticed bright stuff in the cases sparkling in a way I wasn't used to seeing. There were three clerks, all women, but no sign of the tall, ugly, charming man. Two of the clerks busied themselves with other customers. The third made eye contact with me. Her eyes glowed a rare hazel color—too rare. She smiled in a courteous but deferential fashion, then dropped her gaze to her hands, clasped loosely over her belly. A tinge of disappointment ran through my mind when she looked down. Those eyes! After a moment, she looked back at me, and I realized she wore contact lenses.

I pretended to look around the shop and noticed there weren't any price tags. Another one of those places where, if you have to ask, you can't afford it. After a few minutes of what I hoped looked like serious consideration, I approached the hazel-eyed girl and mumbled a few words about wanting to see something. She walked with me back to the case I had been looking at and unlocked it. I pointed to several items at random and she placed them on a red velvet pad on top of the case. She looked over them as she explained them.

I missed part of what she said, as I noticed a dark stripe on the part line of her short bottle-blonde hair. She also wore false nails. Nothing cheap, but nothing real either. Even her voice had a nasally, affected tone, like the hollow sound that pressboard makes when you tap it, as opposed to the thump of real wood.

". . . this is a popular one because of the arrangement. The other one—here, you see?—has a more classic arrangement. And this one here has just the single stone, with a classic cut."

"*Hmmm.* I'm looking for an engagement ring." I thought of Belle and how she would hate everything about this place.

"Oh, how sweet!" the girl said in the tone jewelry shop girls always use when there's a hint of romance. Just living out their fantasies like the rest of us, I guess. She wore no wedding band.

"Yes, we've been together now for about a year, and I figured, time to pop the question."

"Oh! Mmmm . . ." said the girl again, smiling and simpering.

"But you know, I'd also like to purchase her a clasp. She often wears a scarf."

"Oh, a scarf! How sophisticated."

I'd scored a bullseye with that one. "Yes, she got into the habit after she lost her hair from chemotherapy."

"Oh!" the girl steepled her hands in front of her mouth and gasped.

"Yes, it was touch and go for a while, but she's a fighter. She told me my sticking by her carried her through. But I think her spirit helped her beat it."

The girl made cooing noises and sniffled, trying to hold back tears as I laid it on pretty thick. She didn't seem to notice.

"Anyway, we were out with our friends the Sloans recently, and my fiancée . . . or should I say soon-to-be fiancée!" I grinned a lopsided grin as fake as the salesgirl's eyelashes. "She was admiring a diamond clasp that Carmen—Mrs. Sloan—was wearing. I don't recall what it looked like. This was a few months ago, and she said it was new. When I asked Lamont about it, he said he'd got it here."

"That's not a problem! I can look up the style in the records and let you know!"

"That would be great. Thanks."

She brushed away a tear or two and said "I'll be just a moment, Mr. . . . um?"

"Dr. Gupta."

"Dr. Gupta. Oh, I'm sorry! I shouldn't have called you 'mister.'"

"No problem." I flashed my winning, albeit fake, smile.

She tripped off to the back of the shop, through a door marked "Employees Only" thinking god knows what. I looked around a little more. The shop had been decorated without many accents. A crown molding around the ceiling, sturdy Berber wall-to-wall carpet, and mirrors completed the ensemble. I studied the other customers too.

One, a woman in her late fifties, couldn't seem to decide between two ruby settings, both the size of cherries. Her husband—a quintessential fat cat if I ever saw one, with his studied, casual dress, bushy mustache, and benevolent gaze—stood by her side looking comfortable and self-assured. Doubtless, he looked the same way when addressing the shareholders at the annual meeting. Unflappable.

The other pair in the store were a much younger woman and her nervous fiancé. He gulped continually and seemed to be calculating in his head what, if anything, he could afford. The woman, on the other hand, quite nonchalantly asked to see larger and larger stones. She had reached almond-sized and seemed to be eyeing the pecan-sized ones with clear and determined intentions. Her beau looked like he might faint or throw up.

Welcome to matrimony, son.

Hazel-Eyes suddenly reappeared from the back room with a sad expression.

I smiled expectantly.

"Dr. Gupta, I've got bad news for you."

"Oh?"

"Yes. Mr. Sloan did purchase a lovely Tiffany clasp about three months ago, but it was a custom setting."

"What's that?"

"It's where the setting's designed for the customer based on a ring or clasp they have chosen, and then the stone or stones provided by the customer are fitted to the setting." This sounded like something she had memorized by heart.

"Oh. So he had the clasp custom made?"

"Yes. It was based on a Tiffany clasp, but he provided the stone or stones."

"I see."

"Yeah, and I don't know exactly where it was designed, cut, or set. We have a number of different designers. And I don't know what diamonds were set into it." She sounded apologetic.

"*Ahhh . . .*"

"Only Mr. Gatz would know and he's not here today."

"Mr. Gatz?"

"Yes, Norman Gatz. He's the owner."

"Oh."

"If you want, I'll take your number and have him give you a call."

"Okay." I recited my mobile number.

"Or maybe if you ask Mr. Sloan, he can tell you?"

"I'll do that. If you could have Mr. Gatz call me, that would be great."

"I sure will!"

"Great! Thanks for your help."

"Of course! I'm so sorry we didn't have the one your fiancée liked. Would you like to look at some of our other custom designs?"

"No, that's okay. She had her heart set on one like Mrs. Sloan's."

CHAPTER 6

I SPENT PART of the afternoon running down the other receipts Carmen Sloan had given me, including a dress designed by someone who's name I couldn't pronounce, purchased from a Rodeo Drive boutique, also with a name I couldn't pronounce. The other receipts proved to be more of the same. I got nowhere, wondering if I might have to learn to speak both French and Italian to solve this case.

The shop clerks weren't much help, in spite of my abundant charm, so I headed back up Santa Monica Boulevard to the 101 with the idea of heading home when my mobile rang. Hoping it was someone I wanted to talk to, I glanced at the caller ID: Cohen. "Hi Josh."

"Hi Digger! How's it going?" His voice boomed through the speaker, distorting it. I had stopped bothering to turn down the volume.

"Not bad. What's up?"

"Not much. Just was wondering if you had heard back from Blake?"

"No. Why?"

"Oh, probably nothing. It's just that he and me and some of the boys get together for poker once a month, and I can't get ahold of him."

"Oh." I couldn't think of anything else to say.

"Aw, well, he's probably out of town or something." An edge, a question in his voice told me he didn't believe that.

"I called a couple of times and left messages, but I haven't heard back."

"Not at all?" I tried to reassure him, realizing that I had failed miserably.

"Nope." Now he sounded worried, his voice raising a notch or two in pitch.

"*Hmmm.*"

There was a brief silence on his end. I could picture him swilling a cola and staring at the ceiling of his office. But then he abruptly changed the subject.

"How's your other case going?" he asked.

"So-so. Why?"

"Just wondering." A pause during which I could hear him breathing more rapidly. "Hasn't called you back, huh?" He didn't need to say who.

"Nope."

"Well, when you talk to him, ask him to call me," he said, finally.

"Will do."

"Thanks. Bye."

"Bye."

Just as I was looking back at the road, my phone rang again. Belle. "Hi honey!"

"*Novio*! How are you?"

"Fine. What's up?"

"Do you want to go to the symphony next week? It's your favorite, Mussorgsky's *Pictures at an Exhibition* at the Phil."

"Sounds great!"

"Okay. I'll call you with the date and time after I gather the tickets."

"Can I pay for mine?"

"Silly *novio*!" She laughed before ringing off.

I reached the 110, but instead of heading east back to Pasadena, I kept on toward L.A., deciding to play a hunch. Fifteen minutes later, I found myself at the main LAPD headquarters, and five minutes later, in the missing persons bureau. No one paid attention to me, so I looked to see if I knew anyone there. Always good to greet an old friend. All the while, I chided myself. What I'd told Josh was true. I never worked on more than one case at a time. Too confusing.

Among the numerous desks, I spotted a face I remembered from some-where and thought I'd chance it. A roly-poly man with thinning hair and a droopy mustache poured over a chart, sweating and drinking black coffee. He reminded me of a walrus. Walters. That was his name. Something Walters. Jim Walters? Fred Walters? Thelonious Walters? Hell's bells. I got close to him and, before he noticed me, glanced at the name on his desk plate. "Mitch? Mitch Walters?"

He turned to look at me courteously wearing that bland expression peo-ple assume when you call them by name and they haven't the foggiest idea who you are.

"Digger Sharma." I held out my hand. "We met a while back on the Sosa case. I'm a PI."

A glimmer of comprehension, if not recognition, came over his jovial face. "Sharma, yeah. Yeah, I remember you." He smiled and shook my out-stretched hand.

I smiled. "I've been hired to find someone, and, you know."

He nodded sympathetically.

"Anyway, I heard someone ran him through down here. I was just won-dering if I could look at the C-file?"

He eyed me for a minute, his head cocked to one side, as if trying to decide whether to believe me. Then he shrugged and said, "Why not?" He stood up from his desk and waved at a chair. "Have a seat. It might take a few minutes. What's the guy's name?"

"Noakes. Alfie Noakes." I spelled it for him.

He pursed his lips. "Odd name," he said, almost to himself. "Well, if you'll just wait here Mr. Sherpa, I'll see what I can do."

"Thanks." I turned it over in my mind. He was right: an odd name. *Noakes*. What nationality would that be? Maybe it was a misspelling of *Knox* or some-thing similar. Maybe originally French, as in *N-apostrophe-Oakes*. How would I know? I didn't seem up to this case, linguistically, so I turned my limited concentration to the Case of Lamont Sloan and his Curious Behavior, also proving to be linguistically challenging.

He'd bought pricey dresses at shops on Rodeo Drive. Then he'd bought an expensive diamond setting from a well-known jeweler. That didn't seem too smart. He struck me as a pretty smart guy. I mean, he must have realized Carmen shopped at these kind of places too. And he never bought her clothes, according to Carmen. Or jewelry.

The story behind the clasp struck me as pretty screwy too. I mean, if he had a mistress in San Francisco, as suggested by the hotel receipts, why not buy gifts up there? Buying locally smacked of risky behavior. Sloan did not strike me as the kind of guy who took risks. Not those kind, anyway. But he had met with Hawkface, who looked pretty shady even by L.A. standards. Another person who looked to be more complicated than I had thought. I mentally kicked myself, realizing I should have tailed Hawkface rather than Sloan. Dammit.

I got a cup of water and sat down again, wondering when the Walrus would be back. Something nagged at my mind and pushed its way into consciousness. Where did I know Walters from? I had said the Sosa case, first thing that had popped into my head, a gut instinct.

Still, gut instincts are right a surprising number of times. Sosa, Sosa . . . where did I know that name from? Something about a wine smuggling syndicate a few years back. The details were hazy, but I had done only legwork. The bulk of the case had actually been handled by a colleague. I had no memory of why Walters had been involved. Hell, he might have been in a different division then. It might not even have been him, just someone who looked like him.

I looked up and saw him gamboling back between the rows of desks and again had a sense that I'd seen him before. He smiled, holding up a blue folder. I smiled back and he gave me the thumbs up.

"Here it is! You can use one of those rooms." He jerked his thumb over his shoulder. "Just bring it back to me when you're done."

"Thanks. I'll do that." I walked over to one of the small rooms lining one wall of the large office. It had a glass window and a door I could shut. A telephone too. Nice.

I glanced at the name on the chart out of habit and then opened it up. There were a few sheets of paper, a computer printout—probably a rap sheet—and a color photograph. Interesting.

I scanned the photo but didn't recognize the face that stared back at me. Thick, square, and pockmarked with ginger hair, gray eyes, bushy eyebrows, and a nose that looked like it had slowed down a fist or two. His mouth neither smiled nor frowned. Pretty much a head shot, so other than a button-down shirt, open at the collar with no tie, I didn't know how he dressed.

The expression, well, *hmmm*. Pensive, maybe. Cool. Something about the eyes was cool . . . actually, unemotional, I decided. He looked like a guy who didn't talk much. He also looked like the kind of guy who knows things about people and maybe has a few secrets of his own. I don't know why I got these impressions, but my impressions often mean something. I just didn't yet know what.

I laid the photo aside and looked over the computer printout. Some demographic info—six foot one, 185 pounds, male, Caucasian, forty-two years old, resides at 1162 South Mission Avenue in Azusa, a telephone number, car model and license—all of which I jotted down on a pad. That was followed by some descriptions and circumstances: *Last seen wearing a blue, short sleeve shirt, khaki pants, tennis shoes. Last seen by a charmer called Jimmy the Snake Alveoli*—that couldn't be a real name—*in early May*. Now June. *Hmmm. Missing for over a month. Occupation: various.*

I read a bit more of the description but found nothing helpful. I turned to the rap sheet, which stretched several pages. He had a record that went back fifteen years. The charges were not surprising: assault, ADW (assault with a deadly weapon), ADW with GBI (grave bodily injury), racketeering, extortion, fraud, blackmail, possession of stolen goods, receipt of stolen goods, sale of stolen goods. He had many charges but had done prison time only twice. Must've had a good lawyer. His time inside brief and minimum security. Strange for a guy with such violent offenses. He'd been clean for about three years before disappearing. Not on probation or parole.

As I read through the rap sheet, other interesting details jumped out. For instance, Mr. Noakes had not always resided in Azusa. He'd actually lived in Oakland for about ten years. There were a few addresses from up there. Nothing fancy but not the bad part of town either. He'd moved to L.A. about five years ago. A couple of addresses here locally. Again, nothing fancy but nothing bad. Also, some of the later charges were blackmail. I guess he learned a little more finesse. Charged by one John McGregor of Marin, who complained he had been approached by Noakes. Noakes had threatened to reveal certain business inconsistencies if McGregor didn't pay him hush money. McGregor had come clean, though.

Hmmm. Marin was kind of a tony place for Noakes to be waltzing around.

Then the connection became clear. McGregor owned McGregor Smelting and Steelworks in San Leandro. Noakes had worked for him as a welder. That meant he knew how to use a blowtorch. I pictured him in a dark, heavy suit wearing a dark, heavy mask with a tinted glass eye slit, wielding his blowtorch like Arnold Schwarzenegger wielded his uber-machinegun in *The Terminator* movies. I also pictured Noakes in a purgatorial setting of caverns filled with flames and the abyss. Clearly, I'd read too much Dante in college.

John McGregor went up in my estimation a few notches. I don't know if I would have turned in Alfie Noakes.

Anyway, the charge of blackmail landed Noakes in the slammer. But he plea-bargained and got a reduced sentence, yada, yada. As I scanned the page, a familiar name arrested my eye. Under the heading of Counsel for the Defendant I saw a familiar name: Lamont Sloan. Unexpected. Why would a guy like Sloan get mixed up with a grifter like Noakes?

I skimmed the report and then moved on to the other pages, most of which were just technical jargon. At the bottom of the pile, I found a psychological assessment. Not odd in and of itself, but I wanted to see who had requested it. The first paragraph made it clear: Lamont Sloan.

I carefully read through the report. Most of it detailed the usual hard-luck story I expected: born to a poor family in Newcastle-upon-Tyne in Yorkshire, England—aha; Noakes was a British name!—grew up a ruffian, emigrated to the US with his family at age thirteen. Lived in Boston for a few years. Then moved to the West Coast in his late teens. Sent out here more like. Probably his family felt a change of coast would do him and his fledgling criminal record good. Well, why not? L.A. is chock-full of people reinventing themselves.

He did have a juvenile record, but those were in the days before computer files, so there were no copies of records from Boston. Instead, I found a synopsis of the complete file. I guess the prosecution hadn't felt it worthwhile to request all of them. A bit odd, but not remarkably so. Sloan must have felt he had enough to go on with his record in the Bay Area to request the assessment, which showed a certain foresight.

How Noakes had avoided going to prison was beyond me. Must have had good lawyers up there too, but he didn't seem all that well connected. Ah, but those were the days before Three Strikes went into effect. And, who knows? Maybe Noakes had one of those baleful appearances and neglected childhood stories that melt the most cynical and stony of hearts and, more practically, those who matter: the jury, the judge, the press.

I was noting the report and trial date so I could look it up in the archives when I noticed that Noakes had gotten some additional testing. On the Wechsler Adult Intelligence Scale (IQ test), he had scored an 80. This puzzled me. I looked at his picture again. An IQ of 80 doesn't mean you spend your day eating purple crayons and making sounds like an orangutan, but it's pretty damned low. Much lower than normal, anyway. Too low for someone moonlighting as a blackmailer.

I looked at the psychologist's assessment summary, diagnosis, and treatment plan. The shrink thought that Noakes had antisocial personality disorder and mild mental retardation. Product of a violent upbringing, unloved as a child, the whole nine yards. There didn't seem to be any medication for Noakes, but intensive psychotherapy was indicated. Yeah, like he would be able to pay for it. He might have insurance through McGregor Smelting and Steelworks in San Leandro, but somehow, I doubted it. Even if he had had insurance, I couldn't imagine that Mr. McGregor would tolerate this kind of rabbit in the cabbage patch for long.

The mild mental retardation diagnosis gave me an idea. I knew Sloan had been a champion of civil rights cases. Maybe he had taken on the case because he believed Noakes hadn't understood what he was doing. He might have been clumsy in putting the bite on McGregor. He had sure underestimated him. One more angle to explore.

All of a sudden, I realized my stomach was growling. The idea of chicken vindaloo sounded good. Either that or corned beef hash. Maybe both? Ah, the laughing genes. You can never escape them.

CHAPTER 7

A COUPLE OF days later, Carmen Sloan sent me a fax with a list of incoming calls to the house as well as a copies of Sloan's bank statements for several months. She called me to make sure I had gotten it.

"I had to lie, you know," she said. "I don't like lying."

"Cry me a river."

"No, really Mr. Sharma, I had to, and I didn't want to."

"Really? Why? I mean why'd you have to lie?"

"The phone company said they usually don't provide that information, unless there are, um, unusual circumstances."

"So."

"I told them someone was crank calling me."

"Quick thinking."

"Then I figured I should get them for at least a couple of months, so I told them it had been going on for about six months."

"Even quicker thinking."

"Thanks. I thought so."

"Lying isn't that hard you know."

"I know. I just don't like it."

"You'll get used to it."

"You can be a real bastard."

"Better than being a fake ba—"

She hung up with a snarl of exasperation.

I couldn't help smiling. The fax didn't tell me much. Not a lot of calls to begin with, and Carmen Sloan had crossed out ones she knew. I noticed four she hadn't crossed out. One in the 510 area code, Oakland, or East Bay at least. Called twice in the last two months. Of the others, one number called only once. The other two called three or four times, each going back several months. None of the numbers showed calls during the same two-month period.

Interesting.

I almost dialed one of them, but then thought better of it. Everyone has caller ID now and I didn't want people to know my number. I looked around the apartment, which doubled as my office, and sighed. It would be nice to make enough so I could rent office space somewhere. Didn't have to be in Pasadena. Could be downtown. Anywhere but here. Don't get me wrong, it's a nice place. Swimming pool, weight room, underground parking. Not what I would have liked, though.

I had to figure out Lamont Sloan's affairs before something happened to Carmen. Something bugged me about the man himself. So clean. Too clean. Also, something about the charmer he'd met. That guy could scare a fifty-dollar hooker. And those purchases. Lamont Sloan struck me as neither stupid nor careless, but too many of the loose ends reeked of stupidity and carelessness.

I then looked over his bank account. Nothing suspicious there, although his income and expenses impressed me. One thing stood out. A check dated about three weeks ago for nine thousand five hundred dollars. The IRS pays attention to any sum over ten thousand. A payment to someone? If so, why a check? Clumsy way to pay someone. Even though banks destroy checks, they always make an image of them. I took a look at the previous two months' statements and saw payments for the same amounts, roughly one month apart. I wondered if Carmen might be able to get copies of the checks' images and made a mental note to ask her. The amount seemed pretty high to be a regular payment for anything. I mean, most people have their mortgage, car payments, utility bills and so forth paid automatically. Why would Sloan pay via check?

The more I thought about it, the more I convinced myself that his image as a crusader for the poor and down-trodden had to be phony. I mean, the guy's a lawyer, fer Chrissakes! Or was I just jealous? Or a guy in need of a drink, whose physiology wouldn't let him have one?

Probably all of the above.

The phone rang. A restricted number. "Hello?" I answered.

"Hello, may I please speak with Dr. Gupta?" A cultured voice.

Momentarily confused, I then remembered the fake name I had given at the jewelry shop. "This is him."

"Dr. Gupta, this is Norman Gatz calling from Norman's Jewelers in Flintridge. About the brooch."

"Oh, yes, Mr. Gatz. Thanks for calling me back."

"Yes. I am afraid I have bad news for you and your wife."

My wife? Guess the message got a little garbled from Hazel Eyes. "Oh?"

"Yes. You see, Mr. Sloan specifically requested that the work be done by a private company known only to himself. I merely brokered the sale. I don't know who made the brooch. I'm terribly sorry." He didn't sound very sorry and had a habit of pausing too long before he replied, as if concerned people wouldn't believe him.

"No worries, Mr. Gatz. I'll just ask Lamont."

"That would be excellent. If I can interest you or your wife in any other settings, please give me a call."

"Will do. Thanks." Disappointed, I tried to think of some other way I could follow this lead, as it seemed my only one. Then I had an idea. Before he could hang up, I quickly asked, "Do you have any idea of the stone's value?"

He coughed politely. "Of course, but it would not be prudent of me to reveal that sort of information."

"Of course," I rejoined, equally polite. "But, surely, a knowledgeable man like yourself would have some idea." Flattery will get you everywhere.

Gatz paused while his professional ethics wrestled with his ego. Fortunately for me, the latter won out. "I would say the stone was worth far, far more than the setting," he finally admitted.

"I see. Well, you've been very helpful, Mr. Gatz. Thank you for your time."

"You're welcome. Good day."

Good day? Who says that anymore? And his habit of deliberating? Very annoying. Seemed a delaying tactic, maybe an occupational hazard. Anyway, my only lead had kicked the bucket. Back to square one.

While consoling myself with a ginger ale and bitters, I pondered the case of Alfie Noakes. Now it seemed the guy hired to find him had himself gone missing. Not officially, but I couldn't take Josh's concern lightly.

I now knew Noakes had a connection with Sloan. I wondered if anyone else knew that. *Hmmm*. Noakes was a thug but maybe he had been more. He'd served time and it seemed he earned some more toughness on the inside. Also, he knew a man named Jimmy the Snake Alveoli. How can anyone who knows people with names like that come to any good? Worth following up at any rate.

The cool of my apartment enticed me to stay, but I needed to make some untraceable calls. You can block your outgoing number by dialing star-67 but I didn't want the person I planned to call to see "number blocked" on his caller ID. So squinting in the glare of the sun, my shirt sticking to my back, I hustled around the corner to my favorite drug store for a fountain soda. Before going in, I ducked into a phone booth, one of the last remaining relics of the landline and few and far between in L.A. Fishing out the sheet with my notes about Alfie Noakes, I dialed the number of the house on South Mission Avenue. A voice answered "*¿Sí?*"

"Um, is . . . Alfie Noakes there?"

"*No habla Ingles.*"

"Oh . . . um, *esta Señor Noakes aqui?*"

"*No*" came out with some other Spanish that I didn't understand but figured meant something like *you've got the wrong number, dipshit.*

I said a quick *gracias* and hung up.

I looked up some previous numbers and tried a few but got nowhere. The first and second, they spoke only Spanish. The third disconnected. The fourth, they spoke a language I didn't even recognize. Tagalog? Vietnamese? Swahili? Time to give up on that angle.

I sipped my fountain soda, ruminating about Belle and everything else going on, and watching the passers-by, wondering where they might be going to or from. Other people's lives always seem more interesting than our own.

Walking back to the apartment, sweltering in the heat and noise and squinting in the glare, I remembered the numbers from Carmen Sloan. Returning to the phone booth, I scanned the slip of paper and, while dialing the first number, realized it was one of the ones I had already called. Comparing these numbers to the others—Noakes's old ones—two of them matched. Interesting. The guy sure moved around a lot.

Suspicious.

I started off with the one number from Carmen Sloan's list that didn't match any of the ones from Noakes's rap sheet. Disconnected.

Then I compared the numbers again. One of them, for one of Noakes's old addresses, had been called three times about six months ago. All the calls matched up with the dates he had lived there. So that made sense.

The other number matched the South Mission Avenue address. Again, the dates jibed. That left the 510 area code number. I hesitated, an odd sensation prickling the back of my neck. Some private eyes call it intuition. I call it an allergic reaction to the starch they use on my shirt collars. I shook it off and dialed the number. It rang four times before someone answered.

A quiet, intense voice said, "Yeah?"

I recognized it instantly. Hawkface. Breathing heavily. Oh, boy. I hesitated for a moment, and then, lowering my voice and making it as raspy as possible, asked, "Is Alfie there?"

A pause. He stopped breathing. "Who's this?"

I tried not to panic and then had a brainstorm. "Jimmy. Who the hell did you think it was?"

Another pause. He exhaled noisily. "What's wrong with your voice?"

"Gotta cold."

Yet another pause. Rapid breathing. I thought he had smoked me. I held my breath in turn.

"Wait a minute," he said.

After a moment, another voice came on the line. Deep and Sonorous.

The voice Sloan had been talking to on the phone a few days ago. "Jimmy?"

"Yeah," I answered.

"Why the hell are you calling? We agreed not to use the phone."

"It's okay. I'm calling from a pay phone."

"You dumb son-of-a-bitch. That doesn't make any difference." He said something to Hawkface and then said to me, "Anyway, Alfie's not here. I thought he was with you."

"Don't use that tone with me, asshole." Waiting, I wondered if I had gone too far.

"Sorry," he finally mumbled.

"It's okay. We're all jumpy. Well . . ." I thought furiously of something plausible to say. Then I had another inspiration. "There's a problem. Something's gone wrong. It's Sloan."

"Fuck," he muttered. "Is he getting cold feet?"

"Yeah. Something between him and Alfie."

He sighed. "Okay. Now what?"

"You wait for him to call," I gambled.

"Okay. We're going to have to dust, though."

"Yeah, and I really need to vacuum," I quipped, immediately regretting it.

He paused while I held my breath, then grunted, then laughed. "Glad to see you're finally developing a sense of humor."

"Yeah . . ."

After a brief pause and some indistinct talk between the two men, Hawkface came back on the line. "Anyone else know?" asked the quiet, intense voice.

"No," I replied.

"Good. Keep it that way." The line went dead.

I walked back to the apartment with an odd image in my head. An image of a tall, hawk-faced man with prominent eyebrows, gold teeth, and a quiet and intense voice haunted me. As did an image of a man with a deep, sonorous voice, short and stocky in my imagination.

I pictured them in one of those rooms you rent by the week, the air conditioning on, their jackets off revealing shoulder holsters. There would be the sounds of tawdry affairs in the other rooms. The two men would be out of that room in ten minutes. Without a trace.

Suddenly spooked, I ran up the stairs to the apartment. Once inside, I locked and bolted the door. I thought about a lot of things. I thought about dangerous men waiting for something. I knew that Sloan and Noakes were mixed up in it. I thought about Sloan, a spotless lawyer, nevertheless connected with all these shady characters. Maybe in over his head. I thought about the lawyer's wife, lovely and a whole lotta trouble. Mostly, I thought about an Englishman a long, long way from his home in North Yorkshire. Maybe he should have stayed there.

CHAPTER 8

A FEW NIGHTS later, Belle and I went to the symphony to enjoy Mussorgsky's *Pictures at an Exhibition,* one of my favorite pieces of classical music. Originally written by the composer as a suite of piano pieces for a friend's art exhibit, the genius of Maurice Ravel rearranged it into an orchestral suite, alternately powerful, moving, beautiful, and amusing. The Los Angeles Philharmonic still performed in their old digs at the Dorothy Chandler Pavilion. Sonically inferior to Geary's Walt Disney Concert Hall, where they eventually relocated, it was nevertheless charming.

I met up with Belle at the box office. She stunned in a silver blue, off-the-shoulder dress of some shimmering fabric with a pale evolving crisscross pattern, somewhere between moonlight and water. I felt distinctly underdressed even in my tuxedo. Needless to say, she charmed, the cynosure of all eyes and blissfully unaware of it. She wore the dress—which must have cost a fortune—simply for her own and my amusement, but it made her the belle of the ball. Pun intended. That didn't stop her from slipping her hand into my trouser pocket and stealing my car keys. I didn't worry. She would return them. We linked arms and promenaded into the music hall, a mysteriously handsome couple.

Needless to say, she booked us seats in a private stall. Our elevated box, angled toward the stage, afforded an excellent downward view of the audience. We people watched, a favorite pastime of ours.

Happily babbling away in her lilting accent about her work on recombinant DNA, Belle declared it cutting edge and brooked no argument to the contrary. I listened to her musical voice and gazed at her lovely dress and soft features. I sometimes tried to figure out what made her so alluring. Not her face, certainly, by any standards rather plain with no real outstanding characteristics. Nor her dull brown eyes, blonde hair, or rather thin lips. But she was one of those women who knows how to tastefully apply a little makeup to enhance her dull, if pretty, attributes. If someone asked you to describe her, you would have had a hard time alighting on anything specific. But you would say she was beautiful.

The conversation had somehow meandered around to smiles. What made them attractive, who had the best smiles, why we smile, why we don't smile enough, and so forth.

"I think someone who smiles comes across as more interesting," she concluded.

"You're right," I replied. "In fact, I don't think I told you, but I tried an experiment while biking last weekend."

"Oh? What?"

"Well, as I rode along the river, quite a few people joined me, biking, walking, running, rollerblading, and such. So I decided to smile at everyone I passed."

"Interesting, *novio*. And what did you discover?"

"It seemed that about half the women I smiled at smiled back at me."

"Because you're so handsome!"

"Ha ha! Maybe. Anyway, some people were too focused to notice, so we can't count them. But among the rest, almost all the children I smiled at smiled back. Only about ten percent of the men smiled back, but most gave me the curt male head nod of acknowledgment."

"What's that?" she asked.

"You know, a short, quick dip of the chin." I demonstrated for her.

"Is that a real thing?"

"Oh, yeah! You could go anywhere in the world and guys do that to recognize each other."

"You mean guys that know each other?"

"No, any guy can do that. It signifies a connection."

"I don't believe you!"

"It's true! I could go to Asia, Africa, Europe, the Middle East, the South Pole, anywhere. If I'm walking down the street and I make eye contact with another guy, no matter who he is, if I just make the quick head nod"—I did it again—"he will do the same."

She thought about this and frowned. "But what does it mean?"

"It's a universal sign of male brotherhood. It conveys the message, 'Hey, you're okay, I'm okay, we're cool.'"

"Oh. I wonder what its purpose is. I mean, in an evolutionary sense."

I thought about it for a moment. "I suppose that, back when we were uncivilized, males who encountered each other always had to worry about one or the other attacking. Maybe it evolved as a way for men to show each other that they weren't going to have to fight."

"Ah, but you say any guy could do it to any other guy, right? I want to see a demonstration."

"Okay." I looked around. Leaning out of the box, I found an easy target, a man sitting in the box ahead of us, chatting with his companion and occasionally peering around. I pointed to him and said, "Watch this."

The next time he looked around, I stared at him. His gaze passed me before returning. I looked away briefly and then looked back. Our eyes met and I gave him the curt head nod. He returned it and continued scanning the audience in an absentminded way.

She laughed and kissed me.

"Oh, *novio*! You're so cute!"

"Aw, you just caught me on a good day."

After a few minutes of comfortable silence, she turned back to me and asked, "How's your case going?"

I brought her up to date, including my pleasant conversation with Norman Gatz and my frightening one with Hawkface.

"Oh, *novio*, you're getting into some tall seas here."

"I think you mean deep waters."

"Maybe. But I don't think your client's husband's having an affair."

"Oh? Why?"

"Like I said before, she would know. Women's intuition. And the clasp you subscribed? I don't think it was for a woman at all. Not for his wife and not for a mistress."

"Really? Why not?"

"You said the setting cost fifteen thousand and the gem even more."

"Yes. Go on."

"A man doesn't give his mistress jewels worth more than the jewels he gives his wife. And you said he didn't give her jewels."

"That's what she said, yeah. But why not?"

"*Culpabilitat.*"

"Huh?"

She pondered for a moment, trying to recall the English word. "Culpability."

"What?"

"No, that's not right. Guilt! Yes, guilt."

"Really?"

"Yes. When a man's having an affair, he might give his mistress gifts but they never are worth more than the gifts he gives his wife. No matter how cruel and obsidian-hearted a man is, he will always feel guilty about cheating on his wife, even if it's unconscious. In fact, usually a man gives his wife jewelry or other gifts *because* he has cheated on her!"

I thought about this. "You might be right."

"Did you ever cheat on your wife?"

"Actually, no."

"But you told me . . ."

"Yes, that's why we divorced, but I never cheated on her."

To her credit, Belle realized she had touched a sensitive nerve and dropped the subject. "I'm sorry, *novio*," she whispered, leaning over to kiss me again.

I took a few measured breaths. "It's okay. I'm okay. It was a long time ago."

She smiled and leaned her head on my shoulder, massaging my neck with one hand as she slipped my program from one of the side pockets of my jacket and hid it in her purse.

I relaxed again and smiled at her. She never looked lovelier. I leaned over to tell her I loved her—which would have been a first—when the house lights dimmed and the audience murmur vanished. After the concert master took the stage to hearty applause and the orchestra tuned to her "A" note, the conductor, Esa-Pekka Salonen, appeared to an even more robust ovation.

He mounted the podium and held up a hand as he fished in his pockets for his baton. A nervous moment drew into a longer stretch as it became clear that the maestro couldn't find his conducting baton. The orchestra and audience seemed to hold their collective breath as this embarrassing situation grew worse and worse.

All of a sudden, a horrifying notion seized me, too awful even to contemplate. Fearing the answer, I turned to Belle and whispered, "You didn't?"

Confused, she whispered back, "Didn't what?" her eyes still on the conductor.

About to ask if she had pinched Salonen's baton, a general sigh made me look up again. He had found it on the podium. With the aplomb of the imperturbable master, he turned to the audience, smiled wryly, and flourished the baton like a saber.

A wave of polite, erudite, and above all, confident, wealth-infused laughter spread through the hall. He bowed in a self-mocking way, which elicited more genuine laughter and scattered applause. He then turned back to the orchestra, raised both hand and baton emphatically, and launched the pliant symphony into the trumpet strains of the strong asymmetrical rhythms of the opening piece, "Promenade."

I turned to apologize to Belle for my unwarranted assumption, but clearly, she hadn't realized what I intended to ask her. Better to just drop it.

CHAPTER 9

EVEN THE LOUSIEST of snoops makes some progress. And I had two cases to double my chances. But undeniable. No closer to Eddie Blake, Alfie Noakes—or for that matter, Lamont Sloan—than to President McKinley.

I reveled in one of those lazy afternoons where you lounge on the couch after lunch and watch the dust motes floating in the sunlight. As they rise, your spirits rise. As they fall, spiraling down to the carpet, your mood follows. Today, they mostly fell through the slanted beams filtering through the blinds. Perhaps a pun in there, something about the blinds leading the blind, but my low energy made thinking hard. A thrum of traffic passed below me, mostly muted by the double-paned glass of my windows and sliding door.

I guess I must have been a little desperate when Carmen Sloan called me a few days after my unnerving encounter with Hawkface and Deep and Sonorous.

Without even saying hello, she said simply, "I want you to give up the investigation."

I laughed. "Kiddo, there hasn't been any investigation. I've been pounding the pavement and a dozen other places for three weeks and gotten exactly nowhere."

"I don't care," she said. "I just . . . it's just that it doesn't matter anymore."

For the second time in a week, the hair on my neck prickled. "Why not?"

"Well . . ." she paused.

I knew she could think fast so I just waited, imagining her lighting up a cigarette.

"Lamont told me what's been going on, and I don't need you anymore."

"Oh?"

"Yes. He . . . *actually,* I confronted him, and he confessed to having an affair."

I laughed again. "You're breaking my heart, Mrs. Sloan."

"What do you mean?" Her voice hardened.

"I mean, I can't imagine your husband telling you anything of the sort."

"How dare you!" she shouted.

"I dunno, Mrs. Sloan. How dare I? You tell me."

A moment of silence. I pictured her taking drag after drag of her cigarette and expelling the smoke. Then she said, very slowly, in a voice only slightly above zero Kelvin, "You are not to investigate this matter any farther Dr. Sharma. Please send me your expense bill."

Doctor? How did she know? Puzzled, I tried to stall her. "Further."

"What?"

"Further. You meant to say *further* and you said *farther*. Just a grammatical, or if you prefer, syntactical error. I thought you should know."

"Fuck you!" she shouted and hung up.

I smiled and treated myself to a home-made ginger ale and bitters to celebrate the success of both the case and my charm. Yum. At least I got the drink right.

As I sipped my concoction, I tried to make sense of things. No way could I believe that Lamont Sloan had told her anything, confronted or not. Certainly not an affair. Carmen lying again. Nothing new there. But why fire me? Two possibilities. Either someone had told her what really was going on and she figured a private eye—even a lousy one—would find out, something she couldn't allow. Or something or someone had frightened her. I couldn't figure out which, so I called her back.

"Mrs. Sloan? It's Digger Sharma. I—"

"What do you want?" she interrupted, her voice laced with anger. "Why are calling me?"

Time for the old oil. "Mrs. Sloan. Carmen..."

She drew a quick breath at my use of her first name.

"Carmen," I soothed. "I know you've asked me to give up the case, but I'm very concerned about you. Your husband's involved in something that, well... *he's* up to no good." Even though I didn't know what.

"Something that *what*, Dr. Sharma?" Again, she called me *doctor*. Odd. I could ask her about it later.

"Please, call me Digger."

"Okay."

"Look, Carmen, I'm not exactly sure what's going on, but it's more than a simple affair. In fact, I don't think he told you that he was cheating on you. I think he said something else."

"What do you mean?" Fear crept into her voice, which cracked. Good.

"Well, I hate to say this without stronger evidence to back up my suspicions."

"Just tell me straight out, Digger. I'm a big girl."

"I think he's involved in something illegal. And dangerous."

She sighed. "I thought that might be it."

"Really?" It was my turn to be surprised.

"Um..." she paused. Another cigarette maybe? At the rate she puffed through them, I should invest in RJ Reynolds.

"Carmen, are you in trouble?" I finally asked.

"No..." Her voice tapered off and the line hummed with silence. A long pause. Too long. Probably lighting another gasper. Maybe I should warn her about the dangers of smoking.

"What's going on?" I prompted her.

"I can't tell you. Or, I mean, I won't tell you. It's for your own good, Digger. Lamont's a very powerful man. I've made the mistake before of trying to... well, you know. I've regretted it. I think the only reason he let me off is I'm his wife. I guess I'm lucky he didn't divorce me."

"You mean something like this has happened before?" This surprised me.

"Well, not exactly like this, but, yes, sort of."

To be honest, she had the hook firmly embedded. Now I had to know the skinny. More than professional curiosity. Downright nosy voyeurism. "Carmen, look. If you are in some kind of trouble, I can help you."

"No, I'm not in any trouble."

"Then why tell me not to work on the case anymore?"

"Because *you* are in trouble."

"Me?" The hairs on the back of my neck tingled once more.

"Yes . . ."

"How do you know?"

"Lamont found out I had hired you."

"What?"

"Well, not you. But he found out I had hired a private investigator."

"How do you know that?"

"He told me."

"Oh." Touché.

"How did he find out?"

"You know how I called the phone company to get a list of numbers he had called from his mobile phone? Well, they called him back and he got suspicious when they told him I was the one who called. Then he confronted me."

"Oh boy," was all I could think to say. "I'm sorry, Carmen."

She sighed.

"Don't be," she replied. "But I'm truly sorry Digger, I really am. I should have been more honest with you from the beginning."

I suppressed yet another "*What?*"but decided instead to keep her on topic. I took a deep breath. "What exactly did he tell you?"

"He . . . a few nights ago, when he confronted me, he said he suspected that I had hired a private dick—that's what he called it—I mean, you."

I smiled. "I've been called worse. Go on."

"He said I'd better get rid of you, otherwise I'd be very sorry I had hired him, that is, you. He said, 'you'll both be sorry,' meaning both of us."

The line hummed again with silence. What more to say?

"So you want me to just drop it?" I asked. "Pretend we never met?"

"Yes, something like that."

"But not exactly that."

She didn't answer for a few moments. Probably biting her lip. Very cute. "I . . . I can't let you get yourself in trouble this way."

Somewhere deep in my intuitive subconscious, I sensed threads of manipulation slowly binding me like the Lilliputians bound Gulliver. Carmen couldn't be as noble as she sounded, stringing me along. I figured I could check this out later, so I adopted a tone of bravura. "Ha! I live for trouble! I drop ice cubes down the vest of fear."

She laughed but then continued in an urgent but subtly false voice, "Digger, I didn't . . . that is, you didn't impress me at first."

I waited.

"But you've impressed me quite a bit since then."

Hmmm. Now flattery. Interesting. I wondered where she was going with it. "Thanks."

"No, really. Lamont was not just angry. He was unsettled, rattled. It takes a lot to do that to him. You must be pretty good to have shaken him like that."

"You just caught me during one of my rare periods of extended sobriety."

"Always the jokes, Digger!" she laughed.

"Adds seconds to my life."

"Well . . . so?"

"So what?"

"Will you drop it?" A tone of concern edged into her voice. For her or me I couldn't tell.

"You really want me to?"

"Yes." This time firmer.

I sighed. "Okay. You win. I'll drop it. But you've got to promise me one thing, Carmen."

"What's that?"

"That you'll call me if *you* get into trouble."

"Okay, Digger. I can promise that."

"Okay, then I'll drop it. One more thing."

"What's that?"

"I can't call you Carmen anymore. From now on, it's Mrs. Sloan."

"Okay. That makes sense."

"You take care."

She said thanks and hung up.

I sat there for some time, the dappled sunlight melting the ice in my drink, trying to think, my thoughts suspended like the dust motes floating lazily down in the sunlight. I couldn't very well continue looking into Lamont Sloan's private affairs, illicit or otherwise. It went against my professional pride to send Carmen Sloan a bill, since I hadn't really done anything for her. However, it went against my principles to starve and not pay the rent, so I wrote up an invoice on the computer, printed it out, and sealed it in an envelope, planning to mail it later.

Too bad, Carmen, I thought. *It would have been nice to see you again.*

The strident ring of my mobile phone broke my reverie. A blocked number, so I answered with a clipped, professional "yeah?" half-expecting to hear Carmen's voice again, thinking that would be nice.

A gruff voice asked, "Is this Digger Sharma?"

"That depends."

"Depends on what?" The voice sounded surprised.

"Whether you're someone I want to talk to."

He laughed. "Oh, you'll want to talk to me all right."

"Yeah?" I tried to sound bored. "Okay, convince me."

"I need to talk to you. In private, like."

I thought about this for a moment. Dangerous. But my only lead in the case. I figured if it looked like I couldn't handle it, I could always call Josh.

"Okay. Where should I meet you?" I finally asked.

"You know the piers in San Pedro?"

"Yeah."

"Just past Pier 74, about a hundred yards maybe, there's a warehouse. Foley's Meats. Meet me there in thirty minutes."

A warehouse? That didn't sound good. Realizing I had no choice, I checked my watch. "Sure. I'll see you there in thirty minutes, Mr. . . . um . . ."

"Alveoli. Jimmy Alveoli."

The hairs on my neck prickled again, but worse than before. Like seeing your kid's daycare center on the evening news.

After I recovered, I said, without (I hoped) a trace of recognition or anxiety, "All right, Mr. Alveoli, I look forward to meeting you. Can you give me any idea of what this is all about?"

He laughed. A gruff laugh to go with his gruff voice.

"It's about a mutual friend of ours, Alfie Noakes."

More tingling. "Okay," I finally sputtered.

We rang off and I changed into a semi-presentable shirt and slacks. I thought for a moment about calling Josh, but then realized I might miss my chance to find Noakes if he showed up. Besides, in broad daylight, what could possibly go wrong?

Famous last words.

I fired up the reliable SMS and hopped on the South 110, the sun glaring down with a vengeful intensity, the rhythms of Prince once again thumping. With light traffic, I made it to San Pedro in twenty minutes and found the warehouse in five. I checked my watch. Five minutes early. No one around, so I decided to do a little advance scouting.

The warehouse itself was quite decrepit. A two-story rectangular building that might have been painted gray at one time, only rust now showed on the walls, and the place had a dingy, run-down feel. I noticed quite a few broken windows on the second floor and my instincts told me that coming here was not such a good idea. At least not coming alone. Let's face it, if a shady character asks you to meet him, an abandoned slaughterhouse ain't the most congenial setting. But hey, a guy's gotta eat.

On the pier to my right about a hundred yards up, some longshoremen unloaded a monstrous freighter called the *La Paloma* out of Malta. To my left, more warehouses like the one in front of me sat idle in various stages of disrepair. Not a popular neighborhood. Apart from the longshoremen up at the freighter, not a soul in sight. Just a few straggly tomcats. One of them meandered over and eyed me as if sizing me up but went back to nap in the sun.

I walked around the whole building. At the back, a small dock jutted out and a ladder disappeared into the water. I had to shade my eyes against the ocean, dazzling in the afternoon sun. Several large ships churned through the calm waters. Lonely horns sounded in the distance, broken only by the shrill cries of seagulls. The cool, salty scent of the ocean wafted around me. Farther out, several yachts cruised effortlessly, their sails billowing in the wind. I wondered if Lamont Sloan had a yacht. I decided I really hated that guy. But I really liked his wife. Maybe in another lifetime . . .

Sighing, I turned to walk back to the front of Foley's Meats, the name stenciled in white on all sides, peeling with age. Even though five more minutes had passed, no one had shown up. I double-checked my watch. Almost forty minutes since the phone call. I waited another fifteen, then decided, somewhat stupidly, to go inside.

I don't know what compelled me to knock on the sturdy iron warehouse door and, after getting no answer, open it. Something told me it might be a lead. As I said my lack of progress made me pretty desperate.

Inside, high walls divided the slaughterhouse into enormous rooms, surrounded on all sides by catwalks. Shadows of machines hulked in each room I passed. I didn't recognize them, but they looked sinister in the dusky light flickering through filthy, yellowed windowpanes. Not surprising, I realized, for instruments of death and dismemberment. The vaguely metallic stench of blood, which had clearly never gone away, assaulted my senses. At first, I almost retched. I've never been able to stand the sight or smell of blood. Judging by the dust and cobwebs, it hadn't been used as an abattoir for a long time.

All of my snooping instincts, including the hair on the back of my neck prickling, pointed to something wrong, while all of my commonsense instincts screamed *get the hell out of here*. My shoes didn't make much noise but my steps echoed loudly throughout the warehouse, making it seem even emptier.

Only it wasn't quite.

Faintly at first—so faintly that I thought it might be my imagination— and then growing steadily louder, I became aware of a humming sound. At first, I thought it might be an engine of some sort. Though I couldn't imagine what powered it. The electricity here had certainly been cut off long ago.

As I followed the sound, it grew in volume. The tone didn't change though, and I wondered what it might be if not an engine. As I passed the large rooms, the shadows and flickering light made me even more nervous. A few times I nudged a wall or tripped over something.

Finally, I came to a smaller room with a concrete floor and pipes running along the ceiling, maybe twelve-by-twelve feet. Along one edge of the room stood a cot. Along the other I noticed a fridge connected to a generator. That solved the mystery of the humming. In the center, a table and several chairs. A TV in the corner.

But I grasped none of that right away; a figure slumped in a chair riveted me. His face was familiar. I'd seen a picture of it once. A thick, square, pock-marked face fringed with ginger hair, gray eyes, and bushy eyebrows. I'd seen all that before. The bullet hole in his forehead was new, however. I looked around the room and then back at the motionless figure, congratulating myself bitterly. I had solved the mystery of the disappearance of Alfie Noakes.

My triumph was short-lived, though.

Someone snuck up behind me very quietly and quickly. I heard only a swishing sound as I turned. A strange sensation of floating, and stars sparkled before my eyes. Then a dark cloud passed over me and I remembered nothing more.

CHAPTER 10

TO SAY I awoke would be misleading. Instead, a series of loosely connected images streamed in and out of my consciousness. One loud voice. Other voices. Lights. Darkness. Pain. Bustling activity. Stillness. More voices. More pain. A dull headache. During one of my moments of lucidity, I heard a familiar voice.

"He whacked you something fierce. Good thing you're so hardheaded!" laughed Josh.

Oh, yes. And Josh. Not at the warehouse, but later, at the hospital. And yes; whoever whacked me whacked me hard as hell. This I know because over the next several, well, days probably, whenever I awoke, I couldn't string two thoughts together.

My head, how it felt. Difficult to put into words. I remembered nothing from before that experience that explains quite how my head felt. Once, Belle told me this about her menstrual period: "It's like your lower body's not attached to your upper body anymore."

That describes it nicely. My head not attached to my body. For a few days anyway. When I could string two thoughts together, I wondered how they'd found Alfie Noakes and me. Turns out one of the longshoremen saw me get out of my car and enter the building. He then saw a car pull around the other side of the building and noticed a man enter the building for just a few minutes before coming out and driving off again. Unfortunately, he couldn't describe the man or his car, other than to say it was a black sedan with tinted windows. After a few hours, he noticed my car still there, so he and his buddies came over to investigate. They called an ambulance and the cops.

Better to be lucky than good.

They discharged me from the hospital after five days. And they had to baby me. I guess I'm not as tough as those old-time, hard-boiled detectives who could take a whack on the head and in a few hours be back to downing martinis and being dragged behind cars. Of course, cars didn't go as fast in those days.

Belle came to visit every day, bless her heart. She came for short visits only, the highlight of my day. I really loved this woman and meant to tell her at the earliest opportunity. Both she and Josh kept asking me what happened, but I could recall very little. I vaguely remembered finding Alfie Noakes and looking around his makeshift digs, but nothing more.

Anyway, I remember gingerly walking out with Belle for her to drive me home from the hospital. I had to walk softly because every footstep felt like walking on my head. Bandaged up like a Sikh, the dressing stood out like a beacon against my dark-skinned face.

A few days later, when my brain could think straight again, I asked Josh how my car—the trusty old SMS—got back in the subterranean garage at my apartment. He had driven it back for me himself. What a nice guy! He also filled me in on the fate of Alfie Noakes.

Apparently, Noakes had been dead a few hours before I stumbled upon him. I've seen a body or two in my line of work, but it never gets any easier seeing someone whose life has been extinguished violently. Cause of death, not surprisingly, gunshot wound to the forehead at close range. The bullet from a .38 revolver. The boys in ballistics tried to match it to records in their database as well as the FBI's, but so far no luck.

There were no other marks on the body, and there were no signs of a struggle. This confused me. Why would a guy with a checkered past like Alfie Noakes allow someone—maybe Jimmy the Snake—to take him to an abandoned packing plant and then sit quietly while being shot? That he had been living there for some time before being killed made more sense.

The same questions puzzled Josh too.

"It usually means one of two things," he explained. "Either they shot him somewhere else and then brought him to the slaughterhouse or he knew the person who shot him well enough to go there willingly and to meet with him periodically."

"The second makes more sense," I concurred.

"I agree."

"With the cot, TV, and fridge it looked like a hideout."

"Not a very good one."

"No." One question still nagged me, especially if Jimmy the Snake had killed Noakes and clobbered me. "Why just bash me in the head? Why not shoot me too?" I asked.

He shrugged. "Dunno. Maybe they were trying to scare you."

"Well, it worked."

At one point while in the hospital, I thought Carmen Sloan came to visit me. But I couldn't be sure; wakefulness and delirium ran together. I knew I hadn't dreamed it because I hadn't dreamed. Not once. That black, empty sleep you have when heavily sedated allows for no dreams. You don't even realize you've been asleep except that it's the next day or hours have passed since you last looked at the clock, but that seemed only a minute ago.

So I didn't know for sure until she called a few days after I got out of the hospital.

"Digger, it's me."

"Hello, Carmen."

"I . . . what? You said you weren't going to call me Carmen anymore."

"Put it down to post-concussive syndrome."

"What?"

"It's what happens for a few weeks after you get hit in the head. That's what the doctor said, anyway. He said my head would hurt. It does. He said I'd forget things. I have. He said I might be inappropriate. I guess that's what I'm doing right now."

"But . . . oh, never mind. It's not inappropriate. You've had a terrible time of it and I feel like it's my fault."

How did she know what happened? Should I ask? Better to play dumb.

"Aw, don't worry about it, kiddo, it's part of the—"

"Don't call me kiddo!"

"Sorry." A pause. I imagined her lighting a cigarette. "I'm sorry, Digger, it's just—I feel like this whole mess is my fault."

"Okay, I'll bite. Why?"

"Well, I . . . I didn't tell you the whole truth."

"Tell me something I don't know."

"Don't use that tone with me!" she snapped.

"Sorry. Go on."

"It's just that I knew my husband wasn't having an affair."

I'd been expecting this but wanted to hear where she went with it. "Oh, really? Why did you tell me you did, then?"

"It would be hard to explain . . . that is, I don't want to talk about it over the phone. Can you come over?"

"Probably better if we just meet somewhere."

"Okay, that's fine with me. Where?"

I checked my watch. About 2:00. I decided to try a gamble. "What's the name of that French place on Fairfax a couple blocks north of Wilshire?"

"You mean *Au Pied du Cochon?*"

"Probably." As I said, languages are not one of my strengths.

"Yes, I could meet you there."

"Say, half an hour?"

"Yes. I'll meet you there in half an hour."

Twenty minutes later I parked across the street from the restaurant. Fifteen minutes after that, Carmen Sloan drove up in a light-blue, late model Jaguar convertible with a tan ragtop and those beautiful sultry curves. Yes, both her and the car. These were the ones with the headlights that looked like narrowed eyes and a grille like the maniacal grin of a virago. Unfortunately, the license plate in the middle made the car look like that buck-toothed girl from Luxemburg someone once sang about. She valet parked in the main lot, looked around, and went inside.

I waited a few minutes to be sure she hadn't been followed, then ran across the street and went in myself. She stood uncertainly, looking out the window. When she saw me, she got an odd look. Happiness mixed with something else not quite as nice.

She came up to me and touched my arm. "I'm so glad you're okay."

"What makes you think I'm okay?"

She shook her head and smiled. "Let's have something to eat. I'm starved."

I glanced at my watch. "Isn't it a little late for lunch?"

"It doesn't matter. I haven't had anything all day."

"Okay, we'll eat lunch and call it afternoon tea."

As the maître de seated us, her subtle perfume drifted lazily across the table.

"Why didn't you want to meet at the house?" she asked.

"I dunno. Why didn't you want to talk over the phone?"

She looked bitter for a moment and then answered, "I've learned the hard way that, well . . ." She waved her hand.

"Yes. Phone calls can be traced," I observed.

She fished her cigarettes out of her purse before realizing she couldn't smoke in the restaurant, reluctantly putting them back. She nodded and looked down at the menu. I hesitated, then decided not to tell her that by calling me on the phone to tell me we shouldn't talk over the phone she had already defeated her purpose. It made no sense to point this out to her. Too intelligent not to realize this, she must have her reasons.

"So what do you have to tell me?" I asked.

"Let's order first."

I sighed and sat back. She didn't look up, so I looked over the menu and chose something relatively inexpensive. After we placed our orders, we looked at each other in silence, the soft tinkle of silverware on fine China and murmured conversations the only sounds. Finally, I smiled and spread my hands out as if to say, okay, what now?

"First, I'm sorry," she began.

"We've done this part. Get to the point."

She flushed. "You certainly can be blunt if you want."

"Yeah. First thing they teach you at detective school."

She looked away and bit her lip.

"Look Carmen, you haven't been square with me since the beginning. Your husband isn't having an affair, and you knew that. And *I* knew that, but—"

Her face twitched and her mouth opened.

"—but I figured there must be something going on," I continued. "So I made a few calls and snooped around a little, just so I could take your money with a clear conscience. Then you tell me to drop the case, saying everything had got sorted out, as much a lie as the first story you told me."

"Look, I said I'm sorry."

"Don't worry about it. Comes with the territory."

"I don't like the idea that I'm part of your territory."

"I was speaking metaphorically."

"Oh." She toyed idly with her fork.

"Never mind. Now, if you could tell me why you lied about your husband, then I'll tell you if I can still help you."

"You mean you don't refuse to work with clients who lie to you?" She seemed genuinely surprised.

"If I did, I wouldn't have much work."

"Oh, so that's how it is."

"Yeah, that's how it is."

She took a deep breath. "Promise you won't hate me?"

"I don't make promises I can't keep. But in this case, I doubt anything you're going to tell me will make me hate you."

"I don't like people not to like me," she said, talking almost to herself.

For some reason, I recalled something I had read once. Something about half the mischief in the world being caused by people who just want to feel better about themselves. This certainly seemed to be a case in point. But I had to say something to calm her nerves. "Look, as long as you're not molesting baby squirrels, I promise not to hate you. Satisfied?"

She nodded. She tried to smile but failed. Again, something rang false that I couldn't put my finger on. Maybe the way she continuously rearranged her silverware. Maybe the way she refused to meet my gaze or kept crossing and uncrossing her arms.

Finally, she looked at me. "Lamont's mixed up in something. Something big. I don't know what, but I'm very worried."

"How do you know this?"

"Oh, the same reasons I gave you for thinking he was having an affair. Receipts for hotel rooms, gifts. Every once in a while, someone will call the house and hang up after I answer the phone. It's just . . ."

I waited silently, arms crossed.

"I'm very worried about him. I don't know how much you know about him, but I don't think he's ever been mixed up in anything illegal before."

I laughed. "Fer Chrissakes, he's a lawyer! That's all he's mixed up in!"

"Don't talk about him that way!" She glared at me. "I meant he's doing something illegal."

"Okay. Sorry. Why do you think it's illegal, whatever he's mixed up in?"

"It's . . . he said . . . he said I shouldn't tell anyone."

"Oh, he told you it wasn't aboveboard?"

She nodded.

"I see now. That's why you called me up and told me to stop snooping."

She nodded again.

"So why are we having lunch?"

"Afternoon tea," she said quietly and smiled.

"Afternoon tea, then." I smiled in spite of myself.

"I wanted to apologize to you for lying. And—don't interrupt me—and I wanted you to help me out a little more."

"Oh? I thought you didn't want me involved."

"I didn't. Or, that is, Lamont didn't." She reached over and grasped my arm, pretty tight at that. "Digger, you have to help him! He means the world to me and . . . and I think he's in over his head, with people who might . . ." She stopped and looked down. She raised just her eyes.

Vintage Bacall! Very impressive. I could feel my heartstrings being not just pulled, but tuned, fretted, and bowed.

"You've got to help him. For me. Please."

I disentangled my arm and stared at her for a moment. "It's a good thing you never went in for acting."

She raised her chin along with her eyes this time. "What do you mean?"

"You're lousy at it."

She flushed again and I thought she might slap me, but she just said quietly, "I don't know who to trust anymore."

Again, something tugged at my heartstrings. I knew from bitter experience I was at my most vulnerable. I gazed across the table at this beautiful woman. She had told me that I—and *only* I—could help her. And what's more, she was a damsel in distress. I don't know why I have a soft spot for women like that, but I do. I don't know why they are drawn to me like a magnet, but they are. I don't know why I help people like Carmen Sloan, but there it was: the Digger Sharma philosophy, the modern Don Quixote. I've never really understood why I do what I do. I just do it because it feels right. Worst reason to do anything.

The waiter came with the food. We ate in silence for a few minutes.

"Carmen," I began.

She looked up again, her eyes glistening.

"If I'm going to help you, you have to tell me the truth."

She looked puzzled again. "But I have. As much of it as I know."

"I know that."

"Then what?"

"You have to tell me exactly what your husband told you."

"Oh." Her voice faded, and we munched away at our salads for a while like a couple of goats, she with her brow furrowed. Kind of cute, actually.

After a few moments, she seemed to make up her mind, and she took another deep breath. "My husband's not really Lamont Sloan."

CHAPTER 11

WHAT?" I CHOKED on my romaine lettuce.

After sputtering to catch my breath and a few sips of water, I asked with disbelief, "You mean you two aren't married?"

"No, we're married. It's just that he's not really who he says he is."

"Well, if he's not Lamont Sloan, then who is he?" I asked, confused.

"His legal name's Lamont Sloan. It's the name on all his diplomas and licenses. It's the name everybody knows him by here in L.A. But he had another name before."

"Carmen, what are you talking about? If his legal name's Lamont Sloan, who cares about his real name? There's plenty of people in L.A. who go by fake names. You should know that."

"I don't mean that. I mean, it's not his name that matters. It's that his real name's . . . well, he did something terrible when he went by that name and wouldn't want anyone to find out."

"Oh, I see. He could lose his job, his reputation?"

"His life." She said this very quietly and then cried equally quietly. The tears real this time.

I didn't know what to say, so I just sat there.

Finally, she pulled herself together and said, "My maiden name's Gomez. You probably already know that."

I nodded.

"I thought you might," she continued. "Anyway, my parents came from Mexico. I still have a lot of family there. I visited quite a bit as a kid."

She paused and looked up.

I nodded again, encouraging her.

"When I was fifteen, I fell in love with a young man. A wild and exciting young man. Pedro." Her eyes flashed in a fetching way as she spoke. "A few years older than me and he ran with the wrong crowd. No one in my family liked him and they forbid me to see him. And, anyway, I grew up in Orange County. My parents were first-generation immigrants in America, the land of opportunity. They wanted me to marry a wealthy doctor or lawyer from L.A. and have very American children, so my family could move away from their roots." She dabbed her mouth with her napkin, which she then folded and unfolded several times.

"But then?"

"But then I don't know what happened. An argument at a bar or something. There was a fight. Pedro's so quick tempered. He said it was self-defense. He killed a man." She held her fork to her mouth but set it down before continuing.

I kept quiet.

"I don't know if you know anything about Mexican justice, Digger, but if a man from a poor family kills a man from a rich family, he would be lucky to get life in prison. More likely, the other man's family would kill him."

"So you helped him. You got him out of Mexico and into the States."

"No, actually, I didn't. That's the funny part. A friend helped him get across the border. In the trunk of a car, maybe. Or maybe with border-runners. I don't know. He never told me. All I know is he's wanted by the Mexican government and he can never go back."

"So you helped him."

"Yes, I helped him."

"You never thought he would run away from you the way he ran from justice?"

"Justice! He would hardly get any justice down there." She shuddered. "I thought of that, but he had changed. When I was a young girl and I knew him in Mexico, he was reckless and didn't care what anyone thought of him. When I saw him that night, though . . . I'll never forget it." A shadow passed over her face.

"I must have been about seventeen and had just gotten home from school. My parents were still at work and my brother played football. I heard a knock on the door. How he got our address, I never knew. But it was him. I knew him right away. The same but different.

"His recklessness, gone. He looked—I don't know—haunted. As if he had grown up all of a sudden and had gotten a lot more serious. I think killing that man made him grow up. It took away most of the things I loved in him so much."

"But you still loved him."

"Yes. I still loved—love—him."

"What happened then? I mean, you couldn't very well take him in?"

"No. I had a little money from working part time to save up for a car. I gave him the money, and he swore on his honor he would repay it. He also said he would use the money to find a place to live, someplace where they don't ask you your name or where you're from. Then he would find a job.

"And he was good to his word. He lived in the barrio for a few years. He worked in the fields. He learned English. He speaks English so well that people don't even hear an accent. He got his GED. Somehow, he got a green card and started getting better and better jobs. Pretty soon he was working in the law offices of some high-powered Hispanic lawyer in L.A. who took him under his wing and adopted him. This man did everything for Pedro. He gave him a new name and got him legalized. He gave him a past. A legitimate past. He even got him a birth certificate. He helped him get plastic surgery so he wouldn't look like, well, himself. It was amazing to me, you know. How much different you can make a young man look. He was light-skinned to start with, so it wasn't very hard for him to pass himself off as just another dark-skinned Californian."

I nodded knowing exactly what she meant.

"That's how he went to go on to college and law school. He got a second chance and made the most of it. He owed everything to that lawyer and he never forgot him. He said that if we ever have kids he'll name one after him," she added wistfully.

I made a mental note to ask why they hadn't had kids.

"Anyway, he saw me as much as he could. In secret of course. He had disgraced his family in Mexico. We knew them. My parents would never have approved if they'd known who he really was. His family thought he was dead. So did mine. No one ever found out. But he kept his word. He paid me back the money I lent him, even though dirt poor. And he stayed faithful to me all those years.

"After he started college we were able to be more open. I was going to Long Beach State at the time. I introduced him to my family as Lamont Sloan. Told 'em that he was going to UCLA and that we met at a party. That impressed them to no end. They never guessed. After he finished law school we got married. Then we moved back down here about eight years ago."

"And?"

"And that's it. No one knows about his past. He's a good man Digger. I love him and I'm so scared something's going to happen to him."

"So what's he involved in?"

"I don't know. He's never been very open with people but always was with me. And then a few years ago he suddenly became more distant and cold. Like you said when we first met. But he still loves me. I know that. I think he's scared something will happen to me."

I sighed. "Looks like I read this all wrong."

"What do you mean?" She smiled a bit.

"Let's just say I didn't give you the credit you deserve."

"I'll take that as a compliment."

"Meant as one."

"Thanks."

"And I like your artwork."

She blushed. "It's not very . . ."

"Good? Maybe. But it's genuine."

She looked away for a moment. "It lets me forget myself. It frees me."

"From what?"

She looked back at me. "What? Oh, never mind. It doesn't matter. It's not important."

I shrugged. "Okay. So what do you want me to do?"

"Protect him, Digger. He could protect himself once. He can't do it now. He's too soft."

"I'm surprised to hear you say that. Isn't a Hispanic man's machismo everything?"

"Don't joke about it Digger. Lamont's a good man. He would never try to be macho after what happened to him as a boy. His own thoughts and memories torture him more than any suffering they could have put him through."

"Even death?"

"Yes. Even death."

"I'll do my best Carmen. I don't know where your information fits in. But you're right that he's in over his head."

"Why do you say that? What have you found out?"

"Let's just say there have been some very odd coincidences. When I got bashed in the head I had just found a man involved with your husband in some shady things. Dead."

"Dead!"

I nodded.

"But Lamont would never—"

"Relax," I interrupted. "I don't think Lamont had anything to do with it. These guys he's mixed up with are very tough and completely ruthless. They killed a man who could have made things embarrassing for them. They didn't hesitate to kill him. I don't think they would hesitate to kill Lamont. Or you."

Her eyes widened.

"You must be completely honest with me now okay?" I continued.

She nodded.

"Have you ever heard of a man named Alfie Noakes?"

Her face betrayed nothing. "No. I've never heard that name." She shook her head twice and then nodded. "I think I'd remember it."

"I think you would too. How about Jimmy Alveoli?"

"That's an odd name."

"I agree. I think he's the one who cold-cocked me. Or one of his hire-lings."

"Well . . ." she furrowed her brow. It was cute. Again. Finally shaking her head she said, "Nope. Haven't heard that name either."

"Those are all the names I know who are involved."

She shook her head again. "Sorry. I don't know them."

"That's that. Any idea what Lamont's mixed up in?"

"Not really."

"Okay. Actually, wait a sec . . . there's one other name. Blake. Eddie Blake."

I knew I'd struck oil when all the color drained from her face.

"Yes! I do know him. How did you know Lamont had hired him?" She clenched a fist.

"I didn't until just now."

She froze but then unclenched her fist, relaxed, and laughed. "Okay Digger. You're good. I concede. Okay?"

"When did Lamont hire Blake?" I asked.

"About three or four months ago. Why?"

"I don't know. Why did he hire him?"

She shrugged. "I have no idea."

"You don't?" I asked, skepticism creeping into my tone.

"No!" She flushed again. "Is there something wrong?"

"There are many things wrong."

"I meant with Blake."

"You've met him?" I asked.

"Of course. Is he all right?"

"I don't know."

"What do you mean you don't know?"

"He's been missing for about three weeks."

She frowned as she digested this. "Missing? Oh my god." She turned pale, steadying herself, but rallied quickly and sat up. She beckoned for a server who materialized instantly. She ordered a scotch. She didn't ask me if I wanted one. "If something's happened to Blake then Lamont will be next." She refused to meet my gaze but fumbled with her purse, perhaps craving a cigarette she couldn't have.

"I agree," I said. "That's why you must tell me why Lamont hired Blake."

"I think to find someone."

"Any idea who?"

"No. Do you know?"

"I think I do."

"Who?"

"Alfie Noakes."

"Did he find him?"

"I don't think so."

"Why don't you just ask Alfie Noakes?"

"Because the last time I saw him, just before someone conked me with an anvil, he had a bullet hole in the middle of his forehead. He wasn't saying much."

CHAPTER 12

I HADN'T BEEN completely honest with Carmen Sloan of course. More like economical with the truth. I had only a vague idea of what was going on and no idea where to look for Blake. I couldn't be sure that Jimmy the Snake or one of his goons had bludgeoned me. That, in fact, didn't make any sense. But nothing made much sense at this point. And that whole story about Sloan's past? Could any of that be true? Maybe Carmen had also been economical with the truth.

Sometimes it helps to jot down some notes. So I fished out a writing pad and made three columns: *True, Maybe,* and *False.* I underlined *False* a few times to make it look thoughtful.

What could be true? That Carmen Sloan had hired me under false pretenses. That Lamont Sloan—Pedro, whoever—had got himself mixed up with some bad guys, one of whom sported a hawkish look and gold teeth. Another guy, Jimmy Alveoli—maybe—called to lure me out to the docks. Another truth: somebody thought a .38-calibre bullet would be better for Alfie Noakes's furrows than Botox. But if it really *had* been Jimmy the Snake who called, why did he stop at killing Noakes? Why not kill me too?

A few days ago, I had asked Josh the same question. He laughed and said, "The criminal mind's a strange creature, Digger. We tried to trace that call but got nowhere. I don't know any more about the caller than I do about the guy who creased your bean. Other than he's strong, left-handed, and someone to be avoided."

Other things I knew to be true: Lamont Sloan or Pedro made a few buys that must have set him back a bit. And they were for ladies' amusements. But not for Carmen. And there seemed to be no other lady that I could find.

On to column number two: *Maybe. Alfie Noakes blackmailing Lamont Sloan.* That made logical sense, although I had no evidence to back it up, other than that the two knew each other. *Carmen Sloan not telling me the complete truth.* Well, duh. Would I ever learn? And finally, *Guys Sloan mixed-up with would not hesitate to kill him or Carmen or me.* Thus, whoever slugged me could not have been one of those shady guys because he didn't kill me. Which made no sense at all. Who was I missing? Maybe Miss Gulch—Frida—had masterminded the whole thing. No one ever notices the hired help.

Of all the people involved only Eddie Blake didn't fit into the puzzle. Oh, yeah, one more thing to add to the *Maybe* column: *Eddie Blake probably dead.*

Gruesome.

What about *False?* Lamont Sloan cheating on his wife? Alfie Noakes still alive? Jimmy & the Chain Gang had played a minuet on my noggin? That I had any clue what was going on? The last was the only one I could answer with certainty. I'd seen Noakes dead so that pretty much iced it.

Okay, so notes aren't always helpful. I glanced over my lists again just to make sure I hadn't missed something. It seemed pretty clear I would have to do two things: figure out whether Carmen had told the truth about Lamont Sloan's past and find Eddie Blake. So I called Josh.

"Digger! You sound better." As usual his voice boomed through the phone.

"Than what?"

"Oh, you know. Better than how you sounded when you last called."

"Josh, I was doped up on morphine and looked like a swami."

"You sure did!" he answered jovially.

"So the effects of morphine have worn off and I feel like hell."

"Gosh I'm awful sorry," he snickered.

"Okay, well I have a couple of questions for you." I said.

"Shoot."

"Any leads on Eddie Blake?"

"Why do you ask?" His tone changed subtly. More guarded.

"I'm still doing a little snooping and I haven't been able to find hide nor hair of him."

There was a strained silence. I could picture him staring at his soda, lost in thought.

Finally I asked, "Josh, what's going on?"

His tone turned edgy. "I don't know Digger. I haven't heard from him in over three weeks."

"Is that usual?"

"Not really. I see him once a month but we usually talk a couple of times in between."

"What do *you* think's going on? Could he be on an extended vacation?"

"Not likely."

"Have you talked to his wife?"

"He's divorced."

"Have you been to his place?"

"Well, you know, with my position and all . . ."

I laughed but without humor. "An honest cop, the rarest of men."

"C'mon Digger, I don't—"

"Forget it, Josh. Joke." Another silence, which I again broke. "You want me to go over and check it out?"

"Absolutely not. 4909 Amar Road in West Covina."

"I'll call you."

"Don't."

One shower and spritz later, the trusty SMS and I were purring southbound on the 39. After a few micromances—a slim gal with short blonde hair in a black Jetta and a busty Latina with purple hair in a green Mustang—I found myself in West Covina. An older neighborhood, built back when they expected the houses to last longer than the annuals. On both sides of the street elms and poplars wafted in the afternoon breeze, still warm, but cooler than earlier. Nice.

I rolled down the windows of the SMS and cruised past 4909 Amar Road before parking a few houses down on the opposite side of the street. Blake owned a simple house, a squared affair, painted in that lime green so popular in the fifties. No car in the driveway. Three steps led up to the small porch, rimmed by a black ironwork fence.

I opened the screen door and knocked quietly. As I waited, I looked up and down the street. There were no kids. School day. Nothing to see. Lots of other houses that looked like this one, a middle-class refuge on the fringes of L.A.

After a few minutes I rang the bell. It sounded inside at a distance. No answer to that either. The house had the feel of a place with no one home. But no old newspapers piled up in the drive, a sure sign that someone had stopped them and gone away. I tried the door. Locked.

After looking up and down the street again I ambled over to the side of the house past some sadly drooping pampas grass and other of the weeds that pass for plants in California. No fences divided the front and side yards, just more cactus and agave plants. I sauntered around the house, my footsteps kicking up dust. In the back I noticed the yellowed lawn hadn't been mowed for months and was mostly dead. A small, forlorn shed leaned against the back fence. The fence itself, a dull rust color made of decrepit wooden panels, extended around the house on three sides. The yard contained nothing else. Spotting a curled-up garden hose I examined it closely. When I tried to straighten it out it cracked.

I surveyed the yard once more but nothing jumped out at me. A quiet Wednesday afternoon, the only sounds the twittering of birds and the ubiquitous hum of traffic on the freeways. You can't go anywhere in L.A. and not hear traffic. Except Carmen's house. The city depends on its great highways the way a body depends on its blood vessels.

I opened the back door screen and knocked first quietly then more loudly. No answer. I tried the doorknob. Locked. No one ever finds unlocked doors except in books. Walking around the other side of the house I skirted more dull plants and a few trees that looked as tired, old, and cynical as Reno hookers. Halfway along the house I noticed a square window about eight feet off the ground. Small but open a few inches. Probably a bathroom window.

I thought maybe if I could get up to it I could probably squeeze through it.

Fortunately the shed wasn't locked. In the dim light the usual garden-shed occupants stood as mute evidence for their owner's lack of attention to gardening. In one dingy corner, shoved underneath a workbench, I found a step ladder. I waved away cobwebs, grabbed the ladder, and jogged back around the side of the house.

If anyone had been watching they wouldn't have seen the most graceful performance imaginable. Climbing the ladder and standing on the top rung, my torso level with the bottom of the window frame, I donned rubber gloves and removed the screen. I then poured myself through headfirst, like one of those smooth bourbons I couldn't drink. Unlike the smoothly poured bourbon, I crashed headlong into the bathtub.

The small window just above the shower-cum-tub gave the room some ventilation. I managed to keep from falling on my head only by clinging to the shower head and, performing some gymnastics that would have made Olga Korbut proud, grabbing the rail that guided the glass shower doors. I eased the rest of the way through the window inelegantly and lowered myself into the tub. I made a lot of noise getting in so I stopped and listened hard for a good few minutes. No sound.

Those few minutes also allowed my eyes to adjust to the dim interior lighting. This happens constantly. It's so sunny in L.A. that whenever you go inside a building it's always darker than outside. I didn't begrudge my eyes those few minutes. They were old pals and I might need them. The scent of cheap perfume, nauseating and erotic, wafted around me.

The house had a fairly simple layout. The bathroom opened onto a short hallway. To the right, the living room and front door. To the left, the back of the house, with three doors. One stood ajar to the bedroom. The one on the left opened to the kitchen with a breakfast area, opposite an open family room. The door at the far end led to the back yard. Ugly orange carpeting ran the length of the house. A musty smell pervaded.

I looked around a bit, trying to get a sense of the place. Sparsely furnished but standard for any bachelor's house: big screen TV with a full surround-sound stereo system. I smiled.

The kitchen was utilitarian to a fault. No dishes in the sink. I looked in the fridge, Not much there. A carton of milk told both my nose and my eyes that it had gone over to the dark side. I took it out to look at the date. A month ago. *Hmmm.* Grimacing I replaced the milk in the fridge.

The bedroom was also pretty bare. Just a queen-sized bed, a couple of dressers, and a nightstand. Nothing on the walls. I glanced inside the closet, full of uninspired clothes. Again, I smelled cheap perfume and wondered if Eddie had a floozy girlfriend or liked hookers. I turned back to the bedroom. Yup, pretty much like my place. I flattered myself that I had better taste. Something about the lamp on the dresser struck me as odd. I tried to turn it on but the bulb was dead. I thought about removing it but realized I'd better make myself an escape route first. I walked down the hall to the back door.

After unlocking it, so I could get out quick if anyone came through the front door, I returned to the bedroom and set to snooping in earnest. I checked all the drawers in the bedroom dressers and the nightstand. Nothing of interest.

Next, I peered into all the kitchen cabinets and drawers. Again, not much of interest. I did, however, find a notepad, which I slipped into my pocket. The bathroom didn't bear examination, but I examined it anyway, having not had a good look at it when I fell into the bathtub. Nothing under the sink except porno mags. Again, a lot like my place. Except the medicine cabinet. I found some lipstick, makeup accessories, and perfume. They must belong to Blake's girlfriend. I made a mental note to ask Josh about her.

Finally, in the living room, which might have doubled as an office at one time, a desk with a computer, monitor, keyboard, mouse, and printer, all at least five years old. Ancient in tech time. I swiped the keyboard and came away with a dusty finger. The computer hadn't been turned on in a while. I clicked the power switch.

While the antique warmed up I looked around the living room. Besides the stereo, TV, and perfunctory lounge chairs, nothing told me much about Eddie Blake. No pictures on the walls, no books on the coffee table. No other furnishings. Plain drapes on the windows. An almost anonymous room.

After a few minutes the computer booted up and I stood at the desk to use the keyboard. An old version of Windows—the loading screen said "95"—asked me for a password. I tried a couple of obvious ones—Blake's address, name, date of birth, and so on—but had no luck. I shut off the computer figuring the police IT folks could crack it if necessary.

After another look around the room and a feel underneath the recliner cushions, I went back to the bedroom. I had a feeling I had overlooked something but couldn't put my finger on it. Then it hit me. The closet. I hadn't done a proper examination of it.

Fairly small, the swinging door opened outwards, revealing a walk-in with several shelves for shoes and racks for clothes. My quick scan earlier had shown me that Blake's taste in clothes was no better than his taste in furniture. Everything in the closet was either nouveaux lounge-lizard or desperate used-car salesman but I needed to do a more thorough search.

I clicked on the light and reached up for a shoebox.

A rattling sound made me freeze.

Someone was trying the back door. The back door I had so conveniently unlocked. The same someone turned the handle and the door creaked opened. Fighting panic I turned off the closet light and pulled the door partway closed. Through the crack I could see most of the bedroom and into the hall.

I held my breath and listened but could hear only the furious pounding of my heart. Realizing I had to calm myself I deliberately slowed my breathing to a normal rate and leaned against the door jamb to keep myself from rocking on the squeaky floor.

After a few moments I calmed down enough to hear the sound of a person—no, two people, two men—rummaging through the house. I assumed men because of the heavy sound of their footfalls. They spoke in low tones. Either two people or one very crazy person talking to himself. I smiled in spite of myself and listened hard but they didn't say much.

After about ten or fifteen minutes they came into the bedroom. Just in case they decided to look in the closet I slipped quietly behind several suits and coats, ignoring the musty scent of cologne and cheap perfume. I froze again as I recognized not just one but both voices. The first, quiet and intense.

Hawkface. The other, Deep and Sonorous.

They snarled at each other, clearly angry, but whether with each other or something else I couldn't tell. At any rate it seemed like they couldn't find what they were looking for and I knew they would check the closet before long. Something told me they wouldn't be very happy to find a half-Irish, half-Indian private dick hiding inside.

I felt around quietly for a weapon—any weapon—but it was too dark in the closet to see. I reached past what felt like a jacket to a shelf where I had seen some shoeboxes. I got a box down and opened it, arming myself with a shoe that seemed strangely light. It would have to do.

After what seemed an eternity one of the men barked something to the other. I raised my shoe and assumed a defensive posture behind the coats. I hoped that if they gave the closet only a cursory look they wouldn't see me. In fact, they'd probably have to be looking for me to find me.

The closet door opened and light flooded in. I stiffened, shoe at the ready.

Just then, a mobile phone rang. The one who had opened the door turned and fished something out of a pocket. I peeked cautiously around the coats but couldn't see him clearly, as he faced the light. Short and stocky. I pulled back behind the coats. He spoke a few words, deep and sonorous. Then he was quiet for a moment and finally snapped his phone shut, replacing it in his pocket. He turned off the light and shut the door, plunging me once more into darkness.

"It's done. Let's go," said Deep and Sonorous.

"But—"

"No buts. Let's get the hell out of here. We've done what we came to do."

"But we need to find it."

"We'll come back later."

A silence. I imagined the two men glaring at each other.

"Oh fuck it," said Hawkface.

Their footfalls died away. I heard the sound of the back door opening and closing.

I let out a breath and realized I hadn't been breathing for several minutes. Still, I waited until I heard the sound of a car start and drive away before venturing out of the closet.

Drenched in sweat, I dropped the shoe and stumbled from the closet, panting heavily.

I went to the bathroom, where I splashed cold water on my face. That felt better. It sounded like Hawkface and Deep and Sonorous were looking for something, something they had good reason to think Blake had hidden. And they hadn't found it. Then something spooked them and they split.

I went over their conversation again in my mind. Deep and Sonorous had said something like they had done what they came to do. What could that be? They clearly hadn't found what they wanted. But he also said they could come back later. Very puzzling.

Getting out of there would have been the smart thing to do, so I went out to the living room, peeked through the curtains to make sure no one lurked out front, and then walked toward the back door. I suppose I could have gone out the bathroom window again but felt the need to be civilized. At the back door I stopped. Even if they came back, I probably had some time to complete my own search. They had obviously been called away for something more important. By whom, though? Maybe Jimmy the Snake. Whatever the reason they wouldn't be back for a few hours. Not with L.A. traffic.

So against all good judgment I locked the back door and returned to the bedroom. Taking a few more deep breaths I searched the closet. I looked behind the jackets, shirts, and polyester pants—just to be sure he didn't have a safe behind them—and discovered a collection of women's clothes. Dresses, skirts, blouses, pants. Some fairly nice ones, actually. I figured they must have belonged to Eddie's girlfriend just like the stuff in the bathroom. I sniffed them and realized they were the source of the cheap perfume. On the shelf with the men's shoes I discovered about a half dozen pairs of ladies' shoes. Pumps and such. He must have a live-in girlfriend. She might prove a valuable source. Then I felt inside each of the shoes and came away feeling sordid.

On the floor I found the shoe that I had grabbed as a makeshift weapon. A red, high-heeled stiletto. It seemed a bit large for a woman, so I placed it next to my own foot. Bigger than my shoe. I guess Eddie must have a thing for large women. To each his own.

As I shut the closet door and studied the bedroom one more time, I realized I hadn't checked the bed itself. After peering beneath it on all fours, I stood up to look behind the headboard. Nothing there. I then searched the bedclothes, which seemed to be dirty. I then lifted the pillows and to my surprise found a Smith & Wesson .38 revolver under one of them. Why did Eddie feel the need to sleep with a gun? I bent down to smell it. A heady scent of gunpowder. It had been fired recently. I couldn't tell if it was loaded but figured it best to leave it under the pillow. I wondered if the two goons had placed it there. Maybe that's what they meant when they said they had done what they came to do.

Frustrated, I looked around the bedroom again trying to figure out if I had missed anything else. I then recalled that something had struck me about the lamp. It hadn't worked when I tried to turn it on. Hawkface or Deep and Sonorous had turned on the overhead and closet lights, so no blown fuse, but they hadn't bothered with the lamp on the nightstand.

I checked the cord. Plugged in. I tried to turn it on again. No luck. At first, I thought the bulb had blown because it looked as if it had burned out. But then I looked more closely. The bulb had an odd, oblong shape, like no bulb I'd ever seen. So I unscrewed it and shook it. A faint rattling inside, but not the sound made by a busted filament.

I walked back to the kitchen, which had the best natural light, and studied the light bulb. I couldn't see what was inside the opaque glass. On a hunch, I tried unscrewing the bottom and it came off in my hand. Kneeling on the rug, I carefully tipped the bulb over. And whaddaya know? Out tumbled a beautiful, sparkling, luxurious diamond clasp.

CHAPTER 13

DAMN, DIGGER!" BOOMED Josh several times, turning the clasp over and over and holding it up to the light. A fair-sized stone, even in his enormous paws. "What do you figure? Three, four carats? Must be worth a fortune."

"A hundred grand, give or take a few bucks." I had calculated this based upon what Norman Gatz had told me.

"A hundred grand for this? Are you kidding? Ten times that amount and then maybe you're in the ballpark." Josh shook his head

"Really?"

"You don't know much about jewels, do you Digger?"

"Should I?" It sounded snippier than I meant it.

"Relax. I mean this diamond alone must be worth more than half a million dollars, not to mention the setting. Especially since it came from someplace ritzy."

"Oh."

"Why did you think it was worth only a hundred thousand?" Josh asked.

I hadn't mentioned to Josh about my visit to Norman's and now didn't seem to be a good time. "Like you said, ignorance."

He looked at me for a moment and shrugged. "Okay."

I felt bad. I couldn't level with my good friend about the clasp without also telling him about Lamont Sloan and a few other things.

"I don't suppose I could have that back?" I held out my hand.

"Are you kidding?"

"Oh."

"Jesus, Digger! Eddie's been missing for weeks! You find a diamond worth a fortune hidden in his house. Hidden so well that two hardened thugs couldn't find it, and you ask me if you could have it back?"

"I suppose 'no' would be the polite response."

"Polite isn't the word for it."

I smiled. "Okay."

He didn't seem to be listening to me, though. "What's going on, Josh?"

He shot a sharp look at me but then looked back at the stone. He finally spoke in a low, measured tone. "I don't know, Digger. I'm just afraid that something might have happened to Eddie, and it might have been over this bauble."

Again he held the diamond up to the light and examined it closely. Sighing, he picked up the telephone and punched in a number. While waiting for someone to pick up, he said, "I'm gonna send this to our guy. He'll be able to tell us what it is, what it's worth, and even where it came from. Hell, with any luck, they might be able to tell us who cut it and where."

"You're kidding?"

"Nope. He's really good." He smiled, knowing he had impressed me.

"I guess I have a lot to learn about the modern criminal."

He laughed. "No. Just his techniques. Your modern criminal's driven by the same things that have always driven criminals: greed, lust, anger, hatred."

"Yeah. By the way, who's your guy?" I asked.

"A jeweler named Norman Gatz."

I tried to hide my surprise that Josh's guy and "my" guy were the same. It must have worked because he didn't say anything.

Someone answered his call and he asked for Norman Gatz. He listened and then said, "Could you please have him call me back? It's urgent." He gave has name and number and hung up.

After a moment of silence, he said, "Hey, speaking of diamonds, what are you doing tonight?"

"Nothing. Why?"

"Would you like to go to the Dodgers game? My seatmate had to cancel."

"I don't know. I don't like football."

He laughed loudly. "Digger, you can be such an idiot!"

Later, I laughed aloud myself, in the car. I am an idiot. I knew the Dodgers were a baseball team but had just forgotten.

Maybe my head hadn't recovered from that knock yet.

CHAPTER 14

THANK YOU FOR meeting with me, Mr. Gatz." I figured if Norman was Josh's guy, it might be worth having another chat with him. Josh had called to ask him to meet with me, telling him I was helping the police with the case.

"My pleasure, Dr. Sharma. What can I do for you?"

"Could you please provide me with a primer on the gem industry?"

If my request surprised him, he didn't show it.

"Ah . . ." He leaned back in his chair and lay his hands crossed over his belly. "Now there's a subject of which I never tire." He leaned forward again and poured himself a glass of water from a carafe, offering me one as well. He then sat back and rubbed his chin for a moment. "Where to start?" he mused, almost to himself.

"What you must realize, Dr. Sharma," Gatz began, "is that a gem or gemstone or jewel's just a piece of mineral crystal that has been cut and polished into a beautiful form that incites *desire*." He spoke the last word in a disturbingly sensuous manner, swishing it around in his mouth the same way some people taste a fine wine. "Jewelry's nothing without the dream," he added.

"The dream?" I asked, puzzled.

"The dream of beauty, the aesthetic, the ideal. When a man purchases his lover a fine piece of handiwork, he's capturing nothing less than his dream of *her*."

"Isn't that a bit far-fetched?"

He laughed. "Ah! Yes, well, perhaps."

I smiled at his amusement.

"So," he continued in a more measured, pedantic tone, "the traditional classification, for which we have the Greeks to thank, distinguishes between precious and semi-precious stones. To a modern jeweler, this is not useful because some semi-precious stones—depending upon rarity, setting, style, and so forth—sell for far more than precious stones. Still, traditionally, diamonds, rubies, sapphires, and emeralds are considered precious stones, while garnets, turquoise, opals, quartz, lapis lazuli, and others are considered semi-precious. Some gems are not actually stones but nevertheless considered valuable, such as pearls and amethyst.

"As I noted, they all start out as crystals, gaining value only by virtue of their cut and polish. The exceptions are non-mineral gems like pearls. Modern gemologists usually distinguish gems by virtue of chemical properties. For example, diamonds are made of carbon, while rubies are composed of aluminum oxide."

"I see. But what determines the value of the raw material?" I asked.

"Ah, there are so many factors involved. Clarity, rarity, defects, beauty, and of course, demand. The lack of a universally accepted standard of value further complicates things. Many still consider an evaluation by the naked eye acceptable although magnification represents a modern advancement."

"But what about the stone that Josh Cohen sent you?"

"Oh, of course. Yes. That's the one we had set for Mr. Sloan. A most impressive gem."

"What makes it so valuable?"

"With respect to that specific stone—a diamond—there are four major aspects to be considered. Color, cut, clarity, and carats, with cut probably the most important consideration. This refers to the quality of the workmanship on the original crystal. Color applies to any aspect of the stone that makes it deviate from colorless, somewhat counterintuitively. The less color, the more valuable. Often the color results from impurities, elements such as boron or nitrogen. The clarity rates how clear the diamond is, usually depending upon inclusions or flaws. Finally, carat measures the weight. Generally speaking, among stones that are equal in cut, clarity, and color, the larger the stone, the more valuable."

"I see. And the stone you had set for Mr. Sloan?"

"That's a gem of the first order, or water, as we call it. An indication of the craftsmanship in its creation. The clarity of the stone allows for the proper dispersion of light. The cut provides the brilliance, that is, how we perceive it. The lack of color allows for scintillation of the light that passes through it."

"The sparkle."

"Exactly," he agreed.

I paused, not knowing how to couch my next question, and not wanting to offend him.

"Mr. Gatz, at the risk of sounding indelicate . . ."

He nodded, encouraging me to continue.

". . . when you are asked to set a remarkable stone like that one, do you ever wonder about it's, er . . ."

"Provenance?"

I laughed. "Yes."

He nodded and glanced away, pausing thoughtfully. "You must understand, Dr. Sharma, the world of gems is a somewhat insular one."

"Meaning?"

"Everyone knows everyone."

"I see."

"We have an informal network that allows us to, uh, share information about gems that might not be quite aboveboard."

"Stolen, you mean."

"If only it were that simple!" He laughed. "The world of highly precious gems is something like the world of fine art. Often pieces are purchased at auction with no one knowing the buyer."

"So there's no cataloguing of the most valuable ones?"

"Not really. Apart from famous gems in museums—and I'm sure you've seen or heard about those, the Hope Diamond and so forth—those in private collections are for the most part uncatalogued. Just as someone might purchase a Picasso anonymously to hang it over his mantlepiece, something to show only his most intimate friends, so might someone purchase a rare gem to display in private."

"So there's no way to tell where Mr. Sloan's gem came from?"

"Well, I wouldn't state it so concretely," he replied

"Oh?"

"We know where the gem was cut. We just don't know to whom it was sold, nor the cost, nor of any of the dealers or previous owners. We know only that it came into Mr. Sloan's possession and that it was not reported stolen or missing."

"Reported? Via your network?" I asked.

"Yes."

I bit my lip, wondering where Sloan might have gotten ahold of his diamond. "How do you know where it was cut?"

"Most diamonds are cut in Amsterdam. The initial cut is, as you might imagine, a delicate operation requiring considerable skill and experience. There are various techniques used to cut and shape diamonds. The cut gem is then fashioned with facets, based upon its intended use."

"How do they know that the raw stone's not from some war-torn country in Africa?" I asked, recalling something I had read recently.

"You mean blood diamonds? Yes, that's a problem. The Kimberley Process is a standard used to ensure diamonds that enter the market are not from countries where violent factions control the production of diamonds and use the proceeds to further their aims."

"Does it work?"

"Mostly."

"I see. But the actual cutting you said is mostly done in Amsterdam."

"Correct," Gatz nodded. "The identification of rough diamonds is often based upon their shape, which can be fairly distinct depending upon where they are mined. Cut diamonds are quite another matter.

"The cutter often etches the diamond with a laser, leaving marks that cannot be seen by the naked eye. It does not affect the value of the stone, incidentally. Many diamond cutters in Amsterdam do this, a bit like Picasso signing a painting. The Lazare-Kaplan company, located here in the US, invented the method. Although marks can be removed, the one on Mr. Sloan's diamond remained visible. That's how I identified it for Lt. Cohen. I observed it when Mr. Sloan originally gave me the diamond."

"I see. Did Mr. Sloan tell you where he got it?"

Gatz pursed his lips, brushed invisible lint from his trousers, and drew himself up to his full height—at least his full height when seated. "We do not make such inquiries."

"I'm sorry."

He relaxed. "That's quite all right."

I turned all he had told me over in my mind. I didn't know where Sloan had gotten the diamond, what he intended to do with it, or its original value. He had it set in a clasp, which he apparently gave to Eddie Blake for some unfathomable reason. Why?

"I've taken up too much of your valuable time, Mr. Gatz. Thank you so much." I got up to leave. He stood as well, and we shook hands.

"Happy to be of assistance, Dr. Sharma." I turned to go but when I reached the door, I thought of one more question. Turning back, I asked, "You said most diamonds are cut in Amsterdam?"

"Yes."

"They must be distributed from there to . . . ?"

"Around the world, Dr. Sharma. Around the world."

"And the mode of transportation?"

He looked puzzled. "Pardon?"

"How do they send the cut stones?"

He pondered my question for a moment. "I suspect most are sent via air courier, as it's fastest and safest."

"Are those shipments catalogued?"

"Probably, but that information would not be available."

"What about theft?"

He nodded. "Oh, yes, occasionally a shipment will be stolen."

"Do you know of any recent thefts?"

He looked surprised. "Actually, a recent theft did occur. How did you know?"

"I didn't. Just wondering. Can you tell me about it?"

He peered at me for a moment, then shrugged. "About three months ago, a robbery, called the Antwerp Diamond Heist, took place in Antwerp, Belgium. With some hyperbole, it has been called the crime of the century." He rolled his eyes. "To be fair, it actually was one of the largest thefts in history. A man named Leonardo Notarbartolo masterminded it. The plan and its execution were ingenious, taking approximately a year and a half."

"Do you mind telling me some of the details?"

"Certainly. Shall we sit down again?"

We sat.

"Mr. Notarbartolo had four accomplices, known as Speedy, the Monster, the Genius, and the King of Keys," he began, as if telling a fairytale.

He must have noticed my eyebrows raised in disbelief, as he added, "Yes, colorful monikers, aren't they? I recall them only because I just read up on the theft. At any rate, Speedy was the one closest to Notarbartolo, the least competent of the thieves; the Monster was an expert lockpicker, electrician, mechanic, and driver; the Genius, an alarm systems specialist; and the King of Keys, one of the best key forgers in the world. He's the only one they never apprehended, and his true identity remains unknown."

"You mean they—whoever they are—caught the other four?"

"Yes. In this instance, 'they' were a web of Interpol and government and local authorities spread out across four different countries."

"Four?"

"Yes. The Netherlands, Belgium, Italy, and France."

"Holland and Belgium I understand, but why Italy and France?"

"Notarbartolo, Speedy, and the Monster are all Italian. They fled to France. Notarbartolo, the mastermind of the heist, belonged to a group known as *La Scuola di Torino,* or the School of Turin. He's currently serving a ten-year sentence for his role in the theft. The value of the stolen diamonds was estimated at one hundred million dollars."

"Wow." Truly a mind-boggling, astronomical sum. "How did they pull it off?"

"Ingenious, actually." Gatz looked wistful, almost as if he wished he had thought of it first. "Notarbartolo, posing as an Italian diamond merchant, rented office space in the Antwerp World Diamond Centre where the theft took place. It's one of the largest diamond and gem depositories in the world. He actually got the idea from a New York-based Serbian criminal named Vojislav Stanimirović, who used the same technique many years ago at the New York Diamond Center.

"Renting office space there accomplished several things. First, they provided him with a tenant ID, which allowed him twenty-four-hour access to come and go as he pleased. Second, it gave him access to the safe deposit box located in a vault beneath the building. He visited frequently during the eighteen months it took to plan the heist, so the security staff got used to him and probably became lax in their surveillance of him."

"So he had access to the vault and no one would question him about being there," I said.

"Exactly."

"What about the theft itself?"

"Again, ingenious. They used camera pens to carry out detailed surveillance of the security systems and vaults over many months. They had to overcome at least four security measures. The first in the vault itself. They hid a small camera above the vault door, apparently difficult to see when the lights were on in the antechamber of the vault. This camera broadcast signals to a sensor hidden in a fire extinguisher. Again, they thought of everything. The fire extinguisher actually functioned, but they hid the electronic sensor inside it in a watertight container."

"My goodness!" I exclaimed.

"Yes," Gatz agreed, "very clever. The camera, of course, captured the combination used by the guards to open the vault itself. So this gave them access to the vault. The next issue was the thermal-motion sensors in the vault itself. Notarbartolo visited the vault the day before the heist, spraying the sensors with transparent women's hair spray so no one would notice it. But the oil in the spray effectively insulated the sensors from temperature changes in the room."

"So the sensors wouldn't alert anyone!"

"Yes, that's right."

I whistled.

"The third security measure were the many security cameras both in the vault and surrounding the bank itself. The King of Keys picked a lock that allowed them access to an empty office building near the Diamond Centre. This building and the Centre shared a small, private garden, which was not under surveillance. From the garden, they were able to use a ladder to ascend to a balcony at the Centre. The Genius used a polyester shield to approach a thermal sensor on the balcony and cover it. He then disabled the alarm on the windows overlooking the balcony, allowing them to enter the building undetected.

"Down in the vault, of course, there were more security cameras. But they covered them with dark plastic bags before turning on the lights. That left just the vault itself. The vault door had a magnetic lock made of two plates. When armed, the plates created a magnetic field, which, if broken, would set off an alarm. The Genius dealt with this by creating an additional plate made of aluminum. He somehow attached this to the other plate, allowing them to remove it whilst retaining the magnetic field. That left just the lock to the vault itself.

"Almost unbelievably, the King of Keys duplicated the vault key, roughly a foot in length. It must have been a perfect replica because he was able to open the vault. He then picked the lock on an internal gate. After switching off the lights, the Monster, working in the dark, located a ceiling panel that housed the wires for the security system. How he did it, we'll never know, but he stripped the wires and rerouted the circuit so it would not be activated, even if the circuit was broken."

"Extraordinary!" I whistled.

"Indeed," he relied, dryly. "They then covered all the heat and light sensors, again working in total darkness most of the time. Apparently, they had created a full-scale replica of the vault where they practiced prior to the actual robbery. Using light sparingly to figure out where to drill, they broke the locks on the lock boxes and stole their contents.

"After an hour of cautiously retracing their steps, they met up with Notarbartolo, who had waited for them in a car, and returned to his apartment with the loot."

I realized I had been holding my breath. "Amazing," I sighed.

"Truly. They even returned after the robbery to steal the video taken by the security cameras to hide their identities. It's unlikely they would've have been caught, except Speedy panicked."

"Oh?"

"Yes. They decided not to remove the diamonds, gold, and other precious gems from Belgium because the risk would have been too high. Even though they executed the heist over a weekend, when it would be less likely that someone would visit the vault, they knew that each morning, the private security team hired to guard the Centre inspected the vault. Transporting the gems would be extremely risky once the theft was discovered, which could be a matter of hours. They could have fled to the Netherlands, the border closest to Antwerp, but for some reason they decided instead to go south, to France. I don't know why they didn't go into Luxemburg or Germany, but they no doubt had their reasons.

"Their plan was to hide the diamonds somewhere in Belgium and remove them later, after they all had fled the country safely and anonymously. After they hid the gems, Speedy and Notarbartolo went to France separately; the others went into hiding in Belgium. In France, Speedy and Notarbartolo agreed to burn all the incriminating evidence—you know documents and such. Speedy panicked though, and instead dumped his evidence in a forest in northern France, confident that no one would find it.

"The weakest link in the chain," I observed.

"Exactly. Needless to say, Speedy blundered. The farmer who owned the forest was hunting there and discovered what he thought was trash, figuring teenagers had dumped it in his woods as they had before. When he looked more closely, he discovered several envelopes with the Antwerp Diamond Centre logo. He called the police, who examined the evidence and envelopes and realized it connected to the heist. They in turn alerted Interpol."

"But how could any of the evidence be linked to any of the men? I thought they had destroyed the video footage."

"They had. A pastrami sandwich brought down the whole enterprise."

I laughed, thinking I had misheard him. "What?"

"They found a receipt for a pastrami sandwich among the evidence. Interpol traced the receipt to a deli in the neighborhood of the bank. When they examined video evidence from the deli, they discovered Notarbartolo had purchased the sandwich there. They then pieced together what happened, leading to the arrests of most of the culprits."

"The power of pastrami," I joked.

"Apparently," he replied.

"And you said their haul was worth one hundred million dollars?"

"Among the diamonds, gold, silver, and other jewelry, yes. Notarbartolo later claimed they had been hired by a diamond merchant to steal about twenty million dollars' worth of valuables in an insurance fraud scheme, but no one believed him."

"Were the diamonds cut or uncut?"

"A combination."

I chewed my lip, thinking. "Is there any chance," I began, looking up at him, "that the stone Mr. Sloan brought to you was part of the heist?"

I could tell my question had shocked him, as his eyebrows shot up. "I would never . . ." he began. He stopped and stared at the floor for several seconds. He then continued, in a quieter voice, "I suppose you are right. We should have checked on that. It never occurred to me. Mr. Sloan is such a . . ."

"A respectable, honest, upstanding, and above all, wealthy client."

He flushed. "There's no reason to assume that tone!"

"I'm sorry," I apologized. "Could you check into it and let me or Josh know?"

"Josh?"

"Lt. Cohen."

"Oh. Of course."

"Thanks. By the way, I'm assuming Interpol recovered all the stolen items?"

Gatz smiled strangely. "But that's the most compelling aspect of the robbery, Dr. Sharma."

"What?"

"They never recovered any of it. The thieves refused to reveal where they stashed it but they told Interpol they were not able to smuggle it out of the country."

"You mean . . . ?"

"Yes. Somewhere out there, probably in a quiet forest in Belgium, lies a hidden treasure worth one hundred million dollars."

I gaped at him.

CHAPTER 15

A COMEDIAN ONCE said that if you're having a lousy day, the best thing to do is go over to your friend's house and ruin their day too. I wasn't sure I could claim Carmen Sloan as a friend, but it was no time to nitpick, so I called her up.

"Carmen?"

"Digger?"

"Yeah. D'ya mind if I come over? I need to tell you a few things. I've got some questions."

"Sure. I'm out back by the pool, painting. Today is the staff's day off so there won't be anyone to let you in. Just come around the side yard when you get here."

I didn't know who "the staff" were but assumed it included at least Miss Gulch, the gardener, and the maid.

The SMS purred along the 101 at a steady ten miles per hour. Even with the A/C on, sweat ran down my back. A haze hung over Hollywood. It looked a lot like the haze that hung over L.A., Pasadena, Glendale, and Burbank. A not-very-clever person might have thought it the same haze.

Ignoring some asshole in a red Mercedes hardtop convertible behind me, who kept tailgating me as though it would make traffic go faster, I laughed at the thought of the look on Josh's face when he first saw the diamond clasp. I don't think I had ever seen him impressed before. Must be something that cops cultivate, that look of cool insouciance.

I veered off at the usual exit and, a few minutes later, my tires crunched down the gravel driveway of 30279 Beverly Glen Road for the second time. Could it be only the second time? It seemed I'd talked to Carmen an awful lot for it to be just twice. Could the place be growing on me? Or maybe just Carmen.

I coasted to a stop and turned off the engine. I knew Sloan wouldn't be there because I had tried to make an appointment with him earlier and his secretary had told me he would be out of town until Friday.

The scent of sage wafted around me when I stepped out of my car. I paused for a moment to watch and listen to the birds twittering. Soothing.

Although Carmen had told me to come around back, I figured it might be a good idea to go to the front door first, just for appearances. I knocked. No answer. There were no other cars. Not outside the house, at least. I then noticed a low hum coming from inside the four-car garage. It sounded like a car running. I waited a moment, but no one opened the garage doors. That didn't make any sense with Carmen in the backyard and no one else home. If they had a chauffeur or someone who washed the cars, surely, they would pull the car out of the garage or at least open the doors. I listened for a moment longer, wondering if I should start worrying.

I walked around to the side of the house, quickening my pace with every step. This took some time because the place was the size of an airline terminal and had more windows than the Chrysler Building. I peered into the house but saw nothing, mostly because of the hedges. I could see more once I reached the side of the house, which was shaded by more elms but had no bushes covering the windows.

There was no one on the side of the house. No one out back, either. I was surprised. I had expected to find Carmen lounging by the pool. The faint humming became more ominous. As I stood there in the hot sun, a sudden and terrible thought struck me. I skirted the swimming pool and jumped up three steps to a veranda with a door that I hoped led to the garage.

I pressed my ear to the door and heard the hollow rumble of a car engine. It had an odd echoing quality and of course I knew the garage door was closed.

The hairs on my neck were prickling again. I figured I should pay attention to them. Stepping back, I took a run at the door with my shoulder. There was a loud thud, mostly from the sensitive soft tissue of my shoulder that now hurt like hell.

Desperate, I looked around for something to use to bash in the door, but all I saw were deck chairs. I sat down on one, rubbing my shoulder. I then whipped out my cell phone and called 9-1-1 and explained the situation. They told me not to enter the garage. But as I sat there with a mounting sense of dread, I recalled something from karate, which I hadn't done for years. They said you never used anything you learned in the dojo outside of the dojo except for a life-or-death situation. I hoped this didn't qualified, but figuring it didn't matter, I stood up.

Squaring myself to the door, I dropped into a fighting stance and with a mighty "kiya!" sent a front kick to the door just above the handle. The force moved the door a bit and made my knee ache like my shoulder. Grimacing, I dropped into a left-sided fighting stance and kicked as hard as I could with the other leg. This time, my efforts were rewarded by a loud crack and the door split around the lock.

I reared back and with a mighty shout kicked the door a few more times. Even after the third or fourth one, the wood of the door had cracked only a bit more and my knees and hips were killing me. So I tried something I hadn't tried at first. I turned the door handle. The door opened easily.

It had been unlocked all along.

I pushed the door open, and a cloud of noxious smoke and fumes billowed out of the garage. I instinctively jumped back. Almost blinded by the smoke, I reached through the door around the corner and felt for the electronic door opener. I found something like a square button and pressed it. The motor hummed and the garage door slowly moved upward. Smoke continued to flow out the door where I stood groping and choking, while a cross-breeze from the back door blew more of it out the front. In the murk, I could see a car. As the smoke cleared, I could see the same light-blue, late model, Jaguar convertible I'd seen Carmen driving, with someone that looked a lot like her slumped against the driver's side window.

Grabbing a few gulps of fresh air from outside, I rushed over to the car and tugged at the door. Locked. The window was open a few inches, so I snaked my arm in and pulled the handle. The door opened and as I struggled not to inhale the fumes, I pulled Carmen Sloan's limp body from the car. By this time, the garage door was all the way up and most of the smoke had cleared, so I dragged her out, coughing and wheezing myself, with tears running down my face and my eyes stinging from the fumes.

Once out on the driveway, I felt for a pulse. None. I listened for the sound of sirens but heard nothing. I had given the address to the dispatcher, but it seemed like an eternity had already passed. I had to do something.

I fought down another wave of nausea and gave a hard thwack to Carmen's chest just below her left breast. Again, I felt for a pulse. None. Holding her nose, I took two very deep breaths and exhaled into her mouth with all the strength I could. I then did ten rapid, forceful compressions on her chest. I then went back to giving her breaths and feeling for a pulse. After another eternity, I felt a pulse. Thready but there. Almost simultaneously, the wailing of a siren rose and fell, growing louder and closer. After a few more breaths and compression sets, Carmen stirred a bit and coughed violently. Then she started to gag. I rolled her over and she threw up, coughing and gasping. I wiped her mouth and face with my handkerchief. Violent coughing racked her body, but she could gasp and greedily sucked in the fresh air.

A moment later EMTs, police, and firefighters surrounded me. Amazing what a little phone call can do.

It didn't take the paramedics long to start an IV, place an oxygen mask over Carmen's mouth and nose, and push a few meds. I sat on the driveway watching this surreal scene, then crawled behind a hedge and threw up so violently I thought it would tear my throat open. After a few dry heaves, I wiped my mouth and rolled over onto the grass.

A face peered over the hedge and asked, "Are you okay?"

I closed my eyes but couldn't speak.

I must have look awful, because the same voice called out to someone, and soon, I too had an IV going and an oxygen mask on. I couldn't think straight. I started sweating and the world seemed to revolve around me. At the same time, I started shivering. A few times, tunnel vision closed in on me, but I never blacked out completely. I don't remember much about the ride to the hospital, though.

My brain became less fuzzy after I had been in the ER for a while. I still felt nauseous, and the nurses very kindly told me not to move for a while. I don't think I could have moved, even if I wanted to.

I dozed off again.

CHAPTER 16

I GUESS I slept for a bit, but it couldn't have been long. The next thing I knew, the jovial face of Josh Cohen, LAPD, smiled down on me.

"What are you doing here?" I rasped, my voice almost unrecognizable.

"Well, I figured it was the least I could do, since you were so good as to call me and tell me where you were." His voice seemed very far away.

"What?" Still groggy, I couldn't focus. "I called you?"

"Sure did!" For some reason, this seemed very funny to Josh. "You meant to call 9-1-1, but you called me. Just as good, though."

"Oh, god . . ." I looked left and right. I lay on a gurney in the hospital. I sighed, closed my eyes, and lay back on the pillow, but then sat up quickly. Bad idea. My head exploded. "Carmen!" I gasped.

"She's fine, just fine. Lay back down, buddy." He gently but firmly pushed me back down.

"Thanks. So I called you. What did I say?" I closed my eyes.

"Only that you needed help immediately and that someone was trapped in a garage with the car running. You gave me the address and everything. Don't you remember that? Maybe you inhaled more smoke than they thought."

I opened my eyes. Josh was still smiling, but I could tell by his furrowed brow how much I had worried him. I groaned and closed my eyes again.

"They say you saved her life," he said.

"*Mmmm . . .*"

"Who is she, Digger?"

"You mean—"

"No, I know her name and that stuff, but what the hell were you doing out at that house? That's not your client is it?"

I nodded without opening my eyes.

"I'm impressed, Digger."

"Why?"

"Real easy on the eyes, that one."

"Oh, fer Chrissakes, Josh."

"Don't worry, old buddy, things are under control."

"What do you mean?" I opened my eyes, then closed them just as quickly, covering them with my hand. They had become exquisitely sensitive to light, even closed.

"Her husband's here."

"What?" Again, I sat up and opened my eyes. Again, very painful. I lay back down again. "But I thought he was . . ."

"Thought he was what?"

"Out of town," I glanced up at him.

He raised an eyebrow, but merely added, "Well, we had to call him, you know."

"Yeah, I guess. Where is he?"

Before he could answer, a doctor opened the door and strolled in. He smiled at Josh, and they exchanged the curt male head nod. I smiled, thinking of Belle.

"I'm Dr. Kleinschmidt," he said, shaking my hand. "You're a very lucky man, Mr. Sharma. I guess that should be, Dr. Sharma. But Mrs. Sloan is even luckier. Lucky you found her and remembered your CPR."

I managed a weak smile. "Yeah, I guess."

He performed an exam lasting several minutes and then said, "you seem to be doing okay now. Probably some smoke inhalation but you should feel better in a few days. By the way, her husband would like to thank you personally. That is, if you're up to it."

I would have preferred to meet the elusive Lamont Sloan, or whoever he was, in a more dignified and impressive manner, but I'd had no luck getting an appointment at his office. I then thought of something crucial. "Have you told him I'm a physician?" I asked.

"No."

"Okay, sure, I'll meet with him. Just don't say anything about that."

"Okay. Great! I'll go get him," he said, and left after another nod to Josh.

Josh looked down at me, his brow arched. "Digger, are you sure you're up for this? I mean . . ." He paused, at a loss as to what to say next.

"Up for what? She hired me, she fired me, and she rehired me. It's not what you think. Anyway, I don't think Sloan knows any of that."

Josh shrugged and lapsed into silence.

A few minutes later, a sharp knock at the door and—finally—I found myself face to face with Lamont Sloan. "Mr. Sharma?" he inquired.

I recognized the smooth voice instantly. "At your service." I sat up and bowed as best as could from the gurney.

Sloan frowned and sat down. He just pulled up a chair and sat down with the confidence of a man who is used to going after and getting what he wants without much effort. Impressive. I studied his face, trying to see evidence of the plastic surgery Carmen had told me about. He did look vaguely Latino, but I couldn't tell.

"My name is Lamont Sloan. I am indebted to you, Mr. Sharma. The doctor tells me that you likely saved Carmen's—my wife's life."

I nodded. Josh shifted a bit, his starched shirt rustling.

"Thank you," Sloan said.

"You're welcome." I replied.

Only the beeping of the IV machine, which had exhausted its bag of fluid, broke the silence. That and the usual hospital noises. Overhead pages, double, triple, and quadruple pings for various codes, a rattling cough from the next room.

"This might sound ungrateful for me to say, given that you saved Carmen . . ." Sloan continued.

I said nothing.

". . . but what exactly were you doing at my home? And why did you go into the garage?"

"Didn't Mrs. Sloan tell you?" I asked, ignoring Josh's eyebrows as they danced like a samba line of caterpillars.

"Tell me what?" Sloan asked.

"My line of business," I replied.

"No. No she didn't."

"I am a purveyor of goods, Mr. Sloan. I own an exclusive line of women's fashions. Mrs. Sloan heard of me through a friend and asked me to come by your home."

"You make house calls?" He sounded incredulous.

"Not *house* calls, Mr. Sloan, *fashion* calls." And then I winked at him in a way that made him blush and draw back a bit.

"Ah. I see," he said, finally.

"Exactly," I replied.

"So you came out to our home to sell. . ."

"Oh, we never call it selling, Mr. Sloan!" I minced as much as I could without lapsing into a stereotype. "We call it showcasing!" I waved my arm with a flourish.

He raised an eyebrow and asked, "So you had never met Carmen before?"

"No. I spoke with Mrs. Sloan only once, when we set up the appointment."

Sloan stood up and paced for a moment, looking confused. He then turned to me and said, "But what made you go around to the back?"

"I saw smoke coming from under the garage door and feared someone might be trapped!" I clasped my hands together and drew them up to my chin. In my peripheral vision, Josh gaped at me, openmouthed. "It was ghastly!" I concluded.

Sloan sat down again and eyed me slantwise for a moment, one elbow on his knee, as if cross-examining a witness. "So you went around the back and rescued Carmen?"

I nodded, trying to look both modest and heroic.

"Well," Sloan said suddenly, standing up, "I guess that explains it. I hope you will forgive my inquisition. I'm very shaken by this." He didn't look very shaken to me. He turned to leave but paused at the door and faced me. "I should like to thank you in a more substantial way, if you are amenable."

I tried a coquettish face, modeled after Bacall. "Oh, Mr. Sloan!"

Sloan flushed crimson, his fists clenched, but he quickly mastered his anger and relaxed. "I meant monetarily, Mr. Sharma."

Drawing myself up to full height, which wasn't much from the gurney, I assumed a dignified, altruistic tone. "Mr. Sloan, I could never accept your money. To do so would be to put a price on human life, which can't be done!"

He stared at me again, then shook his head as if clearing away cobwebs. "I respect your sentiments, Mr. Sharma. My apologies if my offer offended you."

"Not at all."

He stepped out but then leaned back through the door again. "If you don't mind, Mr. Sharma, where did you learn CPR?"

"In the Boy Scouts! I made it all the way to Eagle Scout."

He smiled, more a grimace that didn't reach his eyes. "Of course. Well, thank you again."

Josh could barely contain himself, but I put a conspiratorial finger to my lips and listened closely. After a moment, the sound of Sloan's footsteps vanished down the hallway and I let out a sigh of relief.

"What the hell was all that about?" Josh spluttered.

I laughed aloud. It felt good. I hadn't laughed like that in years.

"Jesus, Digger, what in the world?" Josh laughed too, in spite of himself.

"It's just too funny for words!" I coughed and snorted away for a few minutes, Josh watching me with mixed amusement and alarm. I guess he thought I had finally cracked under the strain of my investigations.

"Josh," I gasped, "I'm perfectly fine. I just made an amazing discovery."

"I sure hope so, 'cause you came across as a first-class queer."

"Do you play chess?" I asked.

"What? Um, no. I mean, I've played a few times. Why?"

"What is the most powerful piece on the board?"

He thought about it for a minute. "The queen, I guess."

"Bingo!"

"Digger, what are you talking about?"

"I'm talking about using the queen to checkmate the king."

Josh shook his head. "I have no idea what you're talking about."

"Soon, Josh, old buddy. Soon."

He shrugged. "Have it your way."

"What time does the game start tonight?"

"The game? Oh, the ballgame! Yeah, it starts at seven. Are you up for it?" He looked doubtful.

"Never better. Great, in fact! I bet the Dodgers kill 'em."

CHAPTER 17

SEVERAL DAYS LATER as I went through my mail, I received a mild shock. Along with a letter from my attorney reminding me about a payment I had already made, I received a bill from the gas company, an application to attend the local junior college for a certificate in wine tasting—useful—and something from the California Medical Board. Opening the last first, I learned someone had recently looked into my medical license. Odd. And surprising. Why would someone do that?

I scanned the letter again, but I was no wiser as to who had contacted the Board about me. Mostly out of curiosity, I called the number on the letter to ask. After a few teleprompts, I got to speak with a live human being.

"California Medical Board. This is Sandy. How can I help you?"

"Hi! My name is Digger Sharma, and I got a letter from you guys saying someone had made an inquiry into my Board profile. Could you please tell me who?"

"Sure. How do you spell your name?"

I spelled it out and she placed me on hold for a couple minutes. "Dr. Sharma? It appears that the request was made by someone called Eddie Blake. Do you know that name?"

Eddie Blake? But that made no sense at all! I decided to fake ignorance. "Um, no, that name doesn't ring a bell." I tried to think quickly. "Did you mail him the information or give it to him over the phone?"

"Oh, we mailed it to him, of course. We don't give out information over the phone." I hesitated, almost making a wise crack to the effect that she just had but then decided not to. A be nice to people day.

"I see. To what address?"

I heard her clicking away at a keyboard. "I have the address. Are you ready?"

I grabbed a pen and note pad. "Yes."

"Okay. 30279 Beverly Glen Road, Beverly Glen, California . . ."

I didn't hear the zip code. I sat for a moment, shocked. The Sloan's address?

"Did you get that Dr. Sharma?"

I started. "Sorry, the connection went bad for a second. Lemme read it back to you to be sure I wrote it down correctly." I read it back and she confirmed the address. "Thanks so much for your help, Sandy."

"You're welcome, Dr. Sharma. You have a good day."

"Thanks. You too." I hung up and sat there stunned for a few minutes.

The address seemed to solidify the connection between Blake and Sloan. But why would Sloan ask Blake to look into my Board profile? And over a month ago, before Carmen had even hired me. She told me Sloan had found out about me, but he knew me even before that.

The inquiry made no sense at all. I could think of no reason Blake would look into my profile if Sloan hadn't asked him to. But why would Blake have the documents sent to Sloan's home address? It would have made more sense for him to have them sent to his own address, or possibly even Sloan's office. As Alice in Wonderland said, "Curioser and curioser."

I then realized that Carmen had called me "doctor" several times. I'd noticed it but brushed it off as insignificant. Until now. Sloan must have told her! Very strange. So he knew about my past just as I knew about his. Had he told Carmen? Or simply told her he knew I had been a physician. But why would that interest him anyway?

Questions, questions. *Hmmm.* I dug out the list I had written after my run-in with the blunt object. I scanned the three columns. *True, Maybe,* and *False.* I could add a few more things now.

When Carmen Sloan recovered enough to talk, Josh—bless his heart, he never told her he knew me—took a full statement that answered at least a few lingering questions.

No, she had not been trying to commit suicide. Someone must have taken her unawares out by the pool. All she remembered was something suddenly covering her mouth and nose, breathing in deeply, a burning sensation in her throat, and blacking out.

Yes, the CSI team had found evidence of a brief struggle on the pool deck, a broken glass, a deck chair on its side, a smashed ashtray, and cigarettes littering the deck. So far, no handkerchief with chloroform, footprints, fingerprints, stray hairs, DNA, or any of those things clever investigators use to solve crimes. No evidence in the driveway of any cars having parked there, other than mine, but then the emergency vehicles had messed things up pretty good. Nevertheless, nobody could figure it out. Had her attacker come and gone on foot? On a bicycle? It seemed unlikely. No other footprints, fingerprints, or anything else in the house other than what they expected to find, such as the staff's, Carmen's, and Sloan's. Of course, no one else was home at the time to witness what had happened.

No, Carmen had no idea who would do something like that or why.

Nothing stolen from the house.

No evidence of a break in.

The toxicology reports found no evidence of chloroform in her bloodstream, nor any other substance that she might have inhaled that had rendered her unconscious. It couldn't be chloroform in that case because it remains detectable for up to several hours in the bloodstream, but little is known about its metabolism.

One curious fact had come out, though: the deadbolt on the door between the house and garage had been locked from inside the house. Carmen couldn't explain why, but it seemed to confuse her. It confused us too. Why would someone drag her into the garage, start the car, leave her to die, and then go back in to lock the door from the inside, having then to leave through the house? It made more sense for whoever had done it to leave through the back door of the garage, go through the backyard, then around the side, as I had done. Maybe they had been worried that she would regain consciousness and try to get into the house? But if so, she could just as easily have opened the garage door. No one could figure that out, either.

Hmmm. I wondered for a moment if maybe Sloan had done it himself. But if so, why? And anyway, he had been out of town. Or had he? Only more questions.

Josh passed along a few other gems. A rag had been soaked in gasoline, stuffed in the tailpipe, and lit. That explained the smoke. I asked him why the whole place hadn't exploded, as always seems to happen in the movies.

"It almost did. All it needed was oxygen, which you kindly provided by opening the garage door. With the back door already open though, there was enough of a cross-breeze to allow the gasses to dissipate. Otherwise . . ." he didn't finish the thought, but he drew his index finger across his throat.

CHAPTER 18

SPEAKING OF GEMS, Norman Gatz, eager to live up to his reputation I guess, had the skinny on the gaudy gimcrack I had found in a few days. The cut was exquisite, done in Amsterdam. The stone, a four-carat diamond of the finest quality, probably came from South Africa. He appraised the diamond alone at well over a million dollars. An independent local appraiser valued it at over one-and-a-half million. A guy in New York City priced it closer to two million. The appraisers delicately hinted that the stone might have been smuggled into the country.

Maybe I should have kept the damn thing.

Best of all, the diamond was part of the loot stolen in the Antwerp Diamond Centre heist. I whistled when I heard those "princely sums" and the gem's "provenance," as Gatz termed it. So Sloan had somehow come by the stone and had Gatz set it before giving it to Blake. Strange. Why?

Under *True*, I penciled in *Someone tried to kill Carmen Sloan.* Under *Maybe*, I wrote *Probably same person who killed Noakes.* And finally, under *False*, I scribbled *Robbery not motive.* Also, under the first heading, I wrote *Diamond worth a small fortune. Thugs knew this.* In the second column, I wrote *Probably smuggled into country.*

I reviewed a note higher up in the list in that same column, I read *Whoever called me to warehouse in San Bruno (saying he was Jimmy Alveoli) also one who cold-cocked me (strong, left-handed).*

I felt I could now make an adjustment to that note in the *False* column: it couldn't be Jimmy or one of his pals; if it had been, I would be dead. Carmen would probably be dead. And Sloan, pretty likely, would be dead as well. That would have made for a lot of dead people. The body count sounded like the ending of *Hamlet*. Grisly. Especially the thought that I could have been one of them. It left a pointed question: Why hadn't Sloan been offed by someone? And another: If it had not been Jimmy the Snake or one of his boys, why had the caller identified himself so?

I wondered if current events were somehow linked to Sloan's past.

Reviewing the list again, it seemed I could fill in a few other blanks. Even though Noakes probably blackmailed Sloan, I didn't think Sloan had killed him. It seemed almost certain that Blake had been killed as well, but not by Sloan either. And then that cock-and-bull story Carmen told about Sloan's past. That had to be as false as a drag queen's eyelashes. I jotted a reminder to myself to check into it.

As for the drag queen himself, I laughed again at the thought. I should have figured that one out sooner—while hiding in Blake's closet, to be precise. It hadn't dawned on me then that the dresses at the back of the closet and the massive high-heeled shoe I had chosen as a weapon belonged to Blake. It helped explain why Sloan had paid Eddie with several dresses and a diamond broach from posh boutiques, gifts that never made their way into Carmen's closets or jewelry collection.

The checks Sloan had been writing every month had to be payments to Blake for something—probably to find Noakes, as Carmen had suggested. But it seemed a lot of money to pay a person to find someone he never found. And it seemed Noakes had been blackmailing Sloan, but the checks weren't made out to him. Josh had looked into that angle.

Maybe Blake got greedy and blackmailed Sloan too? No. More likely the payments had been for his services, not blackmail. And then the huge diamond itself, smuggled into the country. What about that? Payment for services? And why smuggled in? To avoid duties and taxes? To avoid someone connecting it to any of the people involved?

Ah, so many questions. I started doodling on my notepad and then remembered the notepad I had taken from Blake's kitchen. Fishing it from my jacket, I got a pencil and lightly, using the side of the lead, brushed the top sheet, hoping to get an imprint of the last thing written on the pad on the page above.

Nothing. How disappointing! It always seemed to work in the movies.

Sighing, I figured I should probably give the notepad to Josh.

I switched on the television to see how much farther downhill the world had slumped since the last time I turned it on, a periodic habit of mine. It must have been a slow news day because the main story on the CNN crawl related to the Governor of Texas, someone named George W. Bush, who had just announced plans to run for the Republican Party's nomination for the presidency. I assumed he was one of the vile progeny of George H.W. Bush.

I snorted and said aloud to the TV, "That guy'll never win. He's an idiot!"

The TV maintained a dignified silence. I switched it off in disgust and vowed to get my news from *The Economist* from now on.

CHAPTER 19

I CALLED BELLE to tell her what happened.

After the expected scolding for being so foolish—and daring—and her admonitions to be more careful, she changed gears and became more consoling. "But what happened?"

I tried to explain but found I could recall only bits and pieces. "Well, I had to wait until the smoke cleared before—"

"Smoke?" she interrupted. "Why was there smoke?"

"Well, you know, from the exhaust."

"*Novio*, the exhaust fumes given off by a car are colorless and odorless. You wouldn't have seen or smelled them. The smoke had to be from something else."

"Oh, yeah, that's right." I had forgotten about the gasoline-soaked rag. "A rag in the exhaust pipe. Someone had set fire to it. That's where the smoke came from."

"But why would someone do that?"

"What do you mean?"

"I mean exhaust from a car is poisonous. That would have killed her if you hadn't rescued her. Why would someone stuff a burning rag in the tailpipe?"

I hadn't thought about this. I couldn't recall if Josh had said anything about it. "I don't know," I admitted.

She remained quiet for a moment. Unusual. I pictured her in her lab, surrounded by industrial glassware and computers, tapping her teeth with her fingernail.

"It could be . . ." she began, "it could be that they wanted you to find her but make it difficult to rescue her."

"Oh! But why?"

"*Novio*, you told me that you thought she was at risk along with you. Maybe a way to try to take care of both of you. Two stones for one bird."

I laughed. "Two birds with one stone."

"Yes. That's what I said."

I laughed but then thought about her theory. "It's possible," I allowed. "But there must be easier ways."

She sighed. "I guess. I'm just thinking aloud."

"And I appreciate it, honey."

She didn't reply, so I added, "How about dinner tonight?"

"Oh, I can't! I'm going to the movies."

She didn't have to add, with a friend. Good thing I'm not the jealous type.

"How about Saturday?" she asked.

"Sure!"

"Okay. See you then. By the way, the other night was wonderful!"

"Oh?" I tried not to smile.

"Yes! My heartrate went off the roof!"

"Completely off it?"

"Yes!"

"I lo—" I began.

She made a kissing sound and hung up.

I lapsed into a reverie for goodness knows how long, perched on a barstool at the counter in my apartment, listening to Dave Brubeck, when I noticed the clock on the microwave flashing 12:00. Power outage. I reset the clock and then automatically went over to the answering machine to reset it as well. All of the lights were blinking, as they always did when the machine had lost power. Out of habit, I pressed the "play" button, and the machine dutifully rattled through messages from my attorney, my mother, and something called the National Organization for Women, asking for money. All old messages, which I had deleted several days before.

It was still early, so I called mom and got sucked into an hour of the obligatory mother-son chatter. When we finally rang off, I sat down again to collect my thoughts, scant though they were. I looked over my notes again and tried to piece together what had happened over the last three or four weeks.

First, I get hired to snoop into the affairs of a wayward husband. Then I get hired to find someone. The husband turns out not to be wayward, the missing person turns up dead, and it seems that the dead guy might have been blackmailing the husband. And everyone involved seemed not only to know each other but also have mutual friends, mostly of the shadier variety. Then I get bashed on the head, and the wife of the un-wayward husband gets gassed. Oh, yeah, and the guy originally hired to find the missing-but-found-dead guy is now, himself, missing and presumed dead. I didn't hold out much hope for him. There were just too many nasty characters lurking about with guns, blunt instruments, and gasoline-soaked rags.

As I pondered various possible fates for Blake, it occurred to me that Josh or one of his cronies probably searched his place. I called Josh.

"Digger! I had no idea you were such a baseball fan!"

"Not bad for my first game, eh? Whoda thunk they'd pull it out in the last, um . . ."

"Inning?"

"Yeah, inning."

"Well, I've got those season tickets, so anytime you wanna go," he added.

"Thanks." I appreciated his generosity.

"You didn't call up just to say hi, did you?"

"Your deductive powers never cease to amaze me."

"Aw, cut the horseshit." He laughed. "What is it?"

"You guys have been over Blake's house, right?" I asked.

"Yeah. Why?"

"Anything interesting?"

He paused, probably to take a sip of cola. "Look, Digger, I'd love to help you with this, but it's out of my hands now because of what happened to that lawyer's wife."

My turn to pause. I understood Josh's position. There would have to be a quid pro quo. "Listen, if you can meet me at Blake's, I can explain a few things."

"Why should I?" he asked.

"Everything's connected, Josh!" I probably came across angrier than I meant to. "I'm sorry. I mean, what happened to Carmen Sloan, what happened to Alfie Noakes, and what has . . . well, probably what has happened to Blake. They're all connected."

A moment of silence, his eyebrows probably dancing the samba. "I'll meet you over there," he said, finally.

"Sounds goo—" I began.

"Then we're gonna go see Carmen Sloan and get to the bottom of this," he growled. Now he was as pissed off as I was. "Dammit, Digger! If you had told me before . . ."

"I know. I'm sorry. I'll meet you there in half an hour."

He grunted. "Don't bother. I'll pick you up."

Traffic was hell, but Josh drove like an angry Jewish guy mad at his friend. That pretty much summed it up and we raced over to West Covina in just over thirty minutes. We parked across the street from Blake's place on Amar Road under the elms and poplars. The shade felt good. Josh fished a key with a yellow tag from his pocket.

The house looked pretty much the same as before, except for the yellow tape over the front door, the hackneyed "Crime Scene—Do Not Cross" label repeated in black capital letters at intervals. The inside, as far as I could tell, looked about the same too.

It took some time for our eyes to adjust. I headed for the bedroom. Josh followed me silently. I opened the closet, turned on the light, and pulled out some of Blake's louder dresses. Josh raised an eyebrow. I pulled out a wicked pair of FMPs—big enough to fit a man's foot—and he actually smiled.

I walked over to the kitchen answering machine and pressed the "play" button, something I had forgotten to do when I had first searched the place. Josh pulled out a pad and started taking notes.

A message from the phone company about the bill. Another message from SCE, also about the bill. A call from someone called Fisher—who didn't say whether that was his first or last name—called to "just to check in." A couple of messages from Josh and me, and a call from the National Organization for Women asking for money.

How do they get everyone's phone numbers?

Disappointed, I shrugged to Josh, who shrugged back. Then, I remembered my recent power outage, and inspiration hit. I pulled out the power plug, waited about ten seconds, and plugged it back into the outlet, and all the lights flashed on the machine. Reset. I pressed the "play" button.

Though the voice itself was unfamiliar, both of us realized instantly who it belonged to. The Scottish brogue and "this is Alfie" pretty much gave it away. He said something about "the gym," or maybe someone named "Jim," and several mentions of expecting someone named "Laurie" or "Lori." Or it might even have been a last name, such as "Lorre." And twice he mentioned "Sloan," both times calling him "that right bastard." Finally, at the end of the message, Noakes said something about a meeting at dawn.

Josh leaned forward, hooked, his eyes narrow and focused on the machine. With a pat on my back, he pressed "rewind" and we listened to the message again. Noakes very clearly gave the date he had called. More than a month earlier.

Spooky hearing his voice after seeing him dead. I wondered if Josh felt the same way, but if he did, he didn't show it, his face tense with that keen vigilance you see in hunting dogs. Now in his element, he scribbled in his notepad, muttering, "Get this to the boys to listen to it. See if they can get more of the . . ." his voice trailed off.

Finally, after listening to the message a few more times, he smiled at me and gave me one of the nicest compliments I've heard in a long time. "Digger, you are one helluva detective. How did you know to unplug that thing? I mean, a tape recorder I could understand it. But this thing must be digital."

I thought about it. "I spent a summer repairing computers in college," I recalled. "These new digital machines are like computers. When you delete a message, you aren't actually erasing it. You're just marking it to be recorded over. Sometimes, if the machine loses power suddenly, the marking to delete the message gets lost, and you can listen to old messages."

"Well I'll be damned," he muttered. "One helluva a detective."

I smiled.

CHAPTER 20

A FEW MINUTES later, we headed to UCLA Medical Center in Westwood to see Carmen, Josh expertly navigating the rush-hour traffic. Sloan had her transferred there from the County hospital as soon as the doctors felt it safe for her to leave the ICU. In the hour or so that it took us to drive across L.A., through its ever-present haze, I filled Josh in on what I knew. He mostly nodded and listened. He also whistled a few times and shook his head. I left out only Carmen's account of Sloan's—or rather Pedro's—early life, mostly because I hadn't a clue where it fit in. If it fit in anywhere. True or not.

Josh, in turn, filled me in on what he knew.

Well, that is to say, he remained quiet, sighed, and after several false starts, said, "I haven't been entirely on the level with you Digger."

"Join the club. We've got T-shirts," I joked.

He looked at me quizzically, but then I laughed, and he relaxed and laughed too, before conceding, "Okay, you got me! Anyway, I didn't know anything about the Sloans. That's a coincidence. I did know about Alfie Noakes and Eddie Blake though. Noakes had been clean for a couple of years even before he came down here from the Bay Area. But we knew about him. A nasty piece of work.

"Someone hired Eddie to find him," he continued. "I found that odd, because why would a guy like Noakes go missing? Eddie and I tried to figure that out. We guessed that Noakes knew something about someone and had gone to ground, either for his own protection or someone else's. At any rate, Eddie never found him. Not that I know of. The first I heard of it was about a month ago, a week or so before I called you.

"Eddie had a bad feeling about the guy who hired him. We know now that it was Sloan, of course. Eddie couldn't pinpoint what it was about Sloan he didn't like, but he had good instincts. If he didn't trust Sloan, he probably had his reasons. Just to be on the safe side, Eddie called me every few days, both so I could help him with any leads and to be be sure he was okay." Josh's jaw tightened.

"I'm sorry," I said. "I didn't know you and Blake were such good friends." His jaw relaxed.

"Well, we don't know where he is, so I guess we shouldn't assume the worst," I said.

His dark and dangerous expression told me he didn't believe me. "So it was a coincidence that Carmen Sloan hired you to keep tabs on her husband," he said. "Of course, she lied to you about pretty much everything, but what can you expect?"

I turned to face him. "What's that supposed to mean?"

He turned to face me. After a searching glance, he turned back to watch the traffic and said, quietly, "I'm sorry."

I shrugged.

He continued in a carefully controlled voice, "I guess I can understand her not coming to us. But dammit! If she had, well—"

"If she had, Blake might still be alive," I finished his thought for him.

He nodded.

"And possibly Noakes too."

He shook his head. "I don't think so. He seems to have crossed a small-time smuggler, the same Jimmy the Snake Alveoli you told me about."

"Really?"

He nodded again. "Yup. The way I understand it, he tried to blackmail Jimmy. Well, you don't blackmail people like Jimmy."

I sat back, biting my lip. A new but not unexpected twist. "So you think Jimmy the Snake had Noakes killed?"

"I don't know. It's likely, but not for sure."

"And Sloan? What about him? How's he mixed up in all this?" I wondered.

"Well," he faltered, "I don't know how to say this . . . Eddie was my friend, but he . . . he wasn't always, you know . . ."

"On the up-and-up?"

"Yeah. That's why he left the force. A good guy, but he could get stupid."

"Is it possible he might have been blackmailing Sloan?" I asked.

Josh thought about it for a few minutes and then shook his head. "No. Even if he had learned something about Sloan—and let's face it, most wealthy, successful guys have some skeletons in their closet—he wouldn't have blackmailed him."

"What if he learned that Sloan was involved in something lucrative?" I asked, thinking about the Antwerp diamond heist.

After a moment, Josh replied, "He would have wanted a piece of the pie."

"Jesus."

"You said it."

Well, that cleared up a few loose ends. "And Jimmy. A small-time smuggler?" I asked. "Didn't the boys say the diamond might have been smuggled into the country? Gatz told us it was part of that big robbery."

"Yeah. We're looking into that too."

We drove in silence for a bit and then compared notes.

"God, there are so many missing pieces to this puzzle!" I exclaimed.

Josh nodded.

When we got to the hospital, I could see Josh's wheels spinning in high gear. "Well," he said, as we walked through the lobby, "let's see if Mrs. Sloan can finally give us some goddamn straight answers." With Josh, cussing meant serious.

Carmen had a private room of course. Filled with flowers. She smiled when she saw me. If startled to see Josh, she didn't show it. "Mr. Sharma is my savior, you know, Lieutenant."

Josh nodded, smiled, and sat down. I followed suit.

"Or should I say, Dr. Sharma? You should have told me!" She wagged a scolding finger.

"Actually, I've worked with Dr. Sharma before. He's very good at what he does," Josh said.

Carmen's eyebrows shot up in surprise, and she looked between us but said nothing.

We sat for a few minutes in silence, and then Josh, with a delicacy I wouldn't have expected from him, said, "Mrs. Sloan, I need to ask you some more questions."

"I've already told you all I know, Lieutenant."

"I know. I mean, you've told us what you remember about what happened at the house. But I have some different questions."

"Oh?" She tried to look startled but crossed her arms, guarded.

"Why would someone want to kill you, Mrs. Sloan?"

"I've told you. I don't know. As far as I know, I don't have any enemies."

"What about your husband?"

"Why would he try to kill me?" She asked.

Interesting response.

"No, I mean, does he have enemies?" Josh continued. "Your husband. Someone who might try to kill him or you."

"Oh, I see. So you think maybe someone tried to get at him by trying to kill me? Well . . ." She furrowed her brow. It looked as cute as it had the first time I'd seen it. The first time she had lied to me. I forced myself to concentrate.

I noticed Josh wasn't looking at her, focusing instead on his notepad.

"I guess he must have enemies. I mean, the kind of law he practices, you know," Carmen continued, waving her hand in an offhand way.

Josh didn't look up from his notepad. "Is your husband in some kind of trouble, Mrs. Sloan?"

Her head turned toward me, but having anticipated it, my eyes darted toward the window.

"Digger!" she admonished.

Josh looked up. He smiled. "You're on a first-name basis with Dr. Sharma?"

She flushed, angry. "You have no right to talk to me that way, Lieutenant."

Josh stood up quickly. Josh is a big man. Big and scary. His face, dark with anger, made him even more intimidating.

Carmen shrank back, drawing the covers around her, and she stared wide-eyed at Josh for a moment. Then she looked away.

"Mrs. Sloan, your husband is connected to a man who was killed. The man hired to find the man who was killed is missing. The man you hired," Josh nodded at me, "was almost killed. If it hadn't been for him, you would be dead now too." He paused.

I couldn't help but admire the way he infused a heavy weight into his words.

Carmen refused to make eye contact with him.

"That's a lot of people dead and missing, Mrs. Sloan," Josh continued. "I'm sorry if you don't like me or my questions or the way I ask them. But it's my job to figure out what the hell is going on. If I don't, your husband might be the next one to die."

That hit home. Carmen's eyes immediately brimmed with tears that ran down her cheeks. She looked lovely. I wanted to hug her and slap her at the same time.

Instead, I chewed on a fingernail.

Josh and I allowed her to weep silently for a few minutes. She covered her face with her hands, then wiped it with a hand towel from her nightstand. Josh walked over to the door and shut it quietly, then sat down again, waiting.

Finally, Carmen looked up, bright and attractive despite her tear-streaked face. "Okay, I guess I had better tell you the truth." She turned to me. "You too, Digger."

I shrugged, strangely unmoved.

"Lamont has been involved in something. Something . . . I think it's . . . he's in trouble." She paused to collect her thoughts. "I don't know what. Honest I don't." She looked at me and then Josh. "You've got to believe me. You've just got to."

Josh nodded in a noncommittal way. "Go on."

"A few months ago, I accidentally overheard a conversation. Don't raise your eyebrows like that, Lieutenant! It really was an accident. I had to ask him about something, and he was talking to someone."

"On the house phone?" interrupted Josh.

"On his cell phone."

"I see."

"I could only hear his side, but it sounded like the person was trying to get money from him. I don't know why I thought that. Just, you know, the way he answered the questions. Anyway, I got more and more worried about him. He started acting more and more strange."

"How so?" asked Josh.

"Spending more time away from me. I even thought he might be having an affair. But he's not the type. Really, he's not." She smiled at me, and I nodded. "So I thought he might be in some kind of trouble. As I said, going out of town a lot, being really, you know, secretive. After finding those things I gave you, Digger—the hotel slips, the receipts and stuff—I decided to hire someone to find out more but I didn't want to go to the police."

"So you called me," I said.

"Yes." She closed her eyes. I noticed circles under them and she suddenly looked very tired. "Yes. I hoped you might be able to figure out what was going on and, I don't know, maybe help Lamont."

I nodded again.

"Well, as you know, a few weeks later he found out that I had hired someone. Like I told you, he didn't know who, but he found out. I don't know how. He has ways of finding things out. It scares me sometimes. So that's when I told you to drop it."

"But I didn't drop it."

"I didn't know the other case you were working on was somehow connected to Lamont until we met that day in the restaurant. Then I knew he really had gotten himself in trouble."

"Did you ever think of calling us, Mrs. Sloan?" Josh's honest face showed real hurt, his brow creased, difficult to conceal.

She shook her head. "I'm sorry, Lieutenant. I thought about it, but Lamont isn't exactly the most popular guy with the police. Nothing against you personally, it's just . . ."

Josh nodded. "No offense taken. I understand."

"When I knew Lamont was really in trouble, that's when I asked you to protect him." She turned to me. "I never knew it would nearly get you killed! I'm so sorry." She dissolved into tears again.

Josh and I exchanged glances. Then he asked, "Mrs. Sloan, who tried to kill you?"

She shook her head again. "I don't know!"

"Do you think whoever it was will try to harm your husband?"

She looked up, thought for a moment, and then nodded. "That's why he bought a gun."

"Who? Your husband bought a gun?"

"Yes, he bought one a few days ago. He said he would teach me how to shoot. He said he didn't need anyone else's help."

Josh sighed, stretched, and leaned back in his chair. "How can anyone—me, Digger, anyone—help or protect him if he doesn't want it?"

She shrugged. "I know, what I'm asking is ridiculous. Impossible. I'm sorry I've been so stupid."

I went over and put an arm around her. I couldn't resist it, okay? I'm human. Big deal. Okay, I'm also something of an idiot. "Relax. You haven't been stupid. In fact, you've probably been acting more wisely than any of us."

"Thanks." She blew her nose noisily. Even that was cute.

Sensing some awkwardness, Josh cleared his throat. "Well, Digger. I guess we'd better let Mrs. Sloan rest."

I nodded. We both looked at her.

She tried to smile. "I'll be okay. Please try to find out what's going on. Even if you have to get involved, Lieutenant, it's better than something happening to Lamont."

"Yes, ma'am, will do."

We made to leave, but when I reached the door, something jogged my memory. I turned.

"Carmen? Do you know anyone named Laurie?"

She frowned. "I've met a few people with that name, but no one close to us."

"How about Jim?"

Again, she shook her head.

I turned again to leave, then decided to try a shot in the dark. "Carmen, what do you know about diamonds?"

"Diamonds? You mean, like, jewelry? Not much. Lamont knows quite a bit, though. He has an uncle who is in the business. Why do you ask?"

"No reason. No reason at all."

Josh and I walked back to the car in silence. But I could see out of the corner of my eye his eyebrows doing that caterpillar samba again. The hound had picked up the scent.

CHAPTER 21

ALTHOUGH IT WAS hard to leave Carmen Sloan in the hospital, I found it harder still to absorb Josh's barely controlled anger when he called the next day.

"They found Eddie Blake," he growled through clenched teeth.

"Damn. What happened?"

He explained in gruesome detail. Eddie had spent a few weeks rolling along the silt at the bottom of the San Francisco Bay before the tides finally deposited him in more shallow waters. According to the Alameda County sheriff, whose deputies fished Blake out of an estuary between Alameda and Oakland Airport, he came out pretty waterlogged.

I could think of nothing to say.

Following an awkward pause, Josh said, "One thing that doesn't fit. They reckon someone dumped him in the bay a few weeks ago, around the same time you found Alfie Noakes."

"So?" I asked. "You thought he had been hired to find Noakes, didn't you?"

"Well, maybe I'm just . . . I dunno."

"What is it?"

Josh sighed. "Is there somewhere we can meet?"

"Why? Is there something you haven't told me?"

"Uh, yeah, Digger. There is."

Puzzled, I suggested, "How about that diner in Old Town Pass?"

"That place we saw Rob Rio that one time?" he asked.

"Yeah."

"I'll be there around lunchtime."

I poured myself a Ginger Rodgers for a change of pace. I must have been pretty low because I laid the grenadine on heavy as I pondered this latest development.

Ha! Development. Makes it sound like film from a camera.

So Josh had held back on me? Of all the people I thought I could trust. But no point getting bent out of shape. Everyone seemed to be lying to or holding out on me. A wise voice asserted itself: I had been lying to or holding out on a lot of people too. Including myself.

Just at that moment, an envelope slid under the door. With a sense of foreboding, I opened it and found a letter from the apartment manager reminding me of a termite inspection. Ah, those laughing gods. At least the apartment manager shoots straight.

An hour or so later, perched across from a hungry Josh Cohen in a 50s-style diner, I munched away at my lunch. He looked uncomfortable, but I decided not to make it any easier on him. I didn't even offer to buy lunch, eating my cheeseburger, fries, and milkshake in silence. I had to take a lactose pill for the dairy. Another genetic deficiency.

Josh usually talked with his mouth full, food spilling out onto his lap, so I found it odd to see him eat in silence. He wolfed down his grub as if he hadn't eaten in days. He didn't speak until we had finished lunch. Even so, the first thing he asked surprised me. "What do you know about Lamont Sloan?"

"Sloan? I thought we were meeting to talk about Eddie Blake?"

"But I have to know."

"Okay. Sloan?"

Josh nodded.

"Just what I read in his bio. I had never even met him until he came to see us in the hospital."

"Nothing more?"

"Nothing, apart from that cell phone conversation I overheard a few weeks ago at the restaurant. That and Carmen hiring me. But I've already told you all this. What's going on?"

"Are you sure there's nothing you might have left out, maybe to protect someone?"

"Protect who?" I burst out, exasperated by his coyness. "Look, if there's something you want to know, just ask!" I blustered. "Because I don't know what the hell you're talking about."

I wondered if he knew more about Sloan's past, at least the past that Carmen had told me about. I still didn't believe her, and the more I thought about it, her story had to be a crock. The more I learned about Carmen, the more sure I became that she told her stories to lead me away from my path in search of the truth, as far into the woods as possible. Maybe to deflect attention from her. Not just from her past, but her present and future. The more I thought about it, the more I convinced myself she was lying about everything. Again.

Josh interrupted my reverie with a sigh. "Okay. My bad," he finally said. "I just had to know how much you knew about him. I thought maybe Carmen had told you more."

"Why would she? What are you saying?" My face burned with anger again.

"Relax, Digger. I'm not saying anything. Just sit back down and finish your fries. And keep your voice down."

I couldn't ignore the tone of command in his voice. Josh could be imposing. I slouched back, arms folded.

He paused again, his eyebrows working overtime. "Digger, this might be hard to believe—I hardly believe it myself—but Lamont Sloan initially tried to hire Eddie to kill Noakes, not just to find him."

Now it was my turn to gawk. "To kill him?"

He nodded.

"But why?"

"We've already talked about possible motives. You brought up blackmail."

"Yeah, but why would someone hire a private eye, especially an ex-cop, to kill somebody? It doesn't make sense! Lamont Sloan must have known Eddie would refuse."

Josh said nothing. I couldn't read his face.

"Wouldn't he?"

Josh shrugged.

"Jesus," I exhaled, my brain doing the Virginia Reel. "But you're a policeman! Eddie had been one too. He must have known you would do something to—"

"To what?" Josh kept his tone even, but his narrowed eyes warned me to tread lightly.

"To stop him?" I finished lamely.

He smiled briefly and shook his head. "I wish that's how it worked, Digger. I really do. I wish it was that easy. But nothing is, especially not our work. Blake was no cheap trigger. Nope. He went after the big game."

"What do you mean?"

"Well, you know how whenever there is some truly awful crime? Say a guy rapes and murders a twelve-year-old girl and dumps her in a ditch. You know how anger boils inside you, like how could somebody—some animal—be so depraved as to do something like that? And you know how everyone gets up in arms and says the guy should fry?"

I nodded.

"Now, think about this: the guy's guilty, no question about it. But for some reason, he walks. Maybe someone forgot to read him his rights. Maybe the guys who brought him in worked him over. Maybe he got a good lawyer.

"The point is, he walks. Guilty as hell of this disgusting crime, but he leaves court a free man. To go out and do it again."

"What about the Three Strikes law?"

"They have to be convicted first."

"Oh." I nodded.

"Anyway, a lot of people, cops especially, get pissed as hell when one of these scumbags gets off after all our work. It especially ate away at Eddie. When he was a kid, someone murdered his sister. They never caught the killer. He never forgot about that or let up in his work. That's why we had to roll him out of the force. He became a serious liability. He did his work too, um, enthusiastically. Suspects he interrogated sometimes ended up dead. He always claimed self-defense, of course. And anytime we heard about some guilty ass-hole who got off on a technicality, well, an astonishing number of times, they had unfortunate accidents and Eddie had no alibi.

"We covered up for him as long as we could. But a lot of the other guys approved of what he was doing. They thought it was a kind of justice."

"Justice? Justice?" I cried. "Vigilante justice, you mean! That's not true justice, Josh, fer Chrissakes! I can't believe I'm sitting here listening to you talk like this. This goes against everything you stand for! It almost sounds like you supported him." I stared into his earnest face, creased with pain and sadness. "You didn't, did you?"

He sighed. "No Digger. I didn't. Never. I understood why he did what he did, but I never approved of it. In fact, it was me who kicked him off the force."

"I'm so sorry. I didn't know."

He waved his hand. "No, no. Don't worry about it. My own conscience has already given me more grief than you ever could, and he understood why. Never held a grudge. And, as you told me once, it's good to hear the truth from someone who tells it straight."

I smiled weakly and shook my head in despair.

"You don't know what it's like out there, Digger. There's a whole segment of society that decent people—people like you—don't usually see, except when they get robbed or beat up or gunned down." He smirked. "Or bashed on the head."

I had to smile at that. "So Eddie, in turn, beat up and gunned them down? He meted out a kind of justice?"

"Yeah. That's what he did. Or at least that's what he thought he was doing."

"So that's why all the holding back," I mused.

"Among other things."

"Okay, I'll bite. What else don't I know?"

"Three things, probably. Three important things, anyway."

"Only three?" I laughed. "I'm doing better than I thought. Okay, what's thing one?"

"Thing one is that Sloan hired Eddie to kill Noakes."

"Which he seems to have done. Thing two?"

"Sloan has connections to Jimmy the Snake Alveoli."

"Yeah?" I whistled. "Okay, that I didn't know. Kudos. And thing three?"

"Lamont Sloan tried setting up Eddie."

"Setting him up? How?"

"I don't know. Eddie knew, though. He said Sloan wanted him to be the fall guy."

"Fall guy? For what?"

"I don't know. Eddie didn't either." He frowned. "But I think you do."

"Me? But I've already told you all I know!"

Josh laughed. "Now that I don't believe for a second."

"But—"

"Wait! Let me finish. What I'm saying is that you know more about Lamont Sloan than I do. I think there is something about him, possibly something that seems insignificant to you but that could help us figure this out."

He slurped noisily at the dregs of his soda while I studied the remains of my lunch. Nothing connected as far as I could tell—well, nothing I wanted to tell Josh.

"Look Digger." Josh fished out his wallet to pay the tab. "Go home, relax, sleep on it. It'll come to you. Probably when you're least expecting it. I'm sure you know more about this case than anyone. Including Carmen Sloan."

I looked up sharply.

"Yes, Digger. I think she's lying about almost everything. But I think she told you the truth about a few things. Think about it."

I could think of nothing to say but felt his statement merited a concrete reply. "Okay, okay. I will." What had she told me the truth about?

Josh then then flipped the conversation in an unexpected direction. "Why did you go into the detective business, Digger?"

"Whaddaya mean?" I asked. "Why the choice of snoop?" He nodded.

"Well, I remembered reading that the guy who wrote the Sherlock Holmes stories was a doctor, so I figured it couldn't be that hard."

I'm pretty sure you could hear Josh laughing all the way out on South Raymond Street.

CHAPTER 22

THE NEXT MORNING, while pondering what Josh had said, I decided words weren't helpful. I pored over my lists but could make no sense of things. Especially given recent events. Well, when words fail, what about a picture? Isn't a picture worth a thousand points of light or something like that? No. That's not it. A picture's worth a thousand words. For me, a picture's worth maybe twenty words. Twenty-five on a good day. I'm no artist. But Carmen was. I thought about the painting I had seen. Her painting. Clumsy, perhaps. Amateurish, definitely. But it told me so much about her.

Fragmented, or so the painting told me. Trapped? By what or whom? Her husband? Her life? Modern life? Something else? I started to wonder whether she might be emotionally unstable. My instincts told me, probably. Well, more than my instincts. Both Belle and Josh had said pretty much the same thing.

Hmmm.

I couldn't think of anything else to do, so I got a piece of paper and drew a big circle in the middle. Inside the circle, I wrote the name *Sloan*. I crumpled up the paper and made two large circles on new, clean sheet. Inside one I wrote *Lamont Sloan* and in the other, *Jimmy the Snake*. I added *real name Pedro? Mexico?* beneath Sloan's name, even though that part probably wasn't true. Then, a dotted line between them. I then drew four smaller circles around Sloan's and labeled them *Me, Carmen, Blake*, and *Noakes*. All connected with

Sloan via solid lines except for me. I connected only to Carmen.

Wishful thinking perhaps.

Then I drew two more circles around Jimmy the Snake and labeled them *Hawkface* and *Deep and Sonorous*. I then connected all of them with solid lines. There was, almost certainly, a link between Hawkface and Sloan. And between Noakes, Blake, and Jimmy the Snake. And last, Blake had killed Noakes, and someone had killed Blake. Oh yeah, and somebody tried to kill me—twice—and Carmen. It was all pretty confusing.

I reached for my book to read but couldn't focus. So I closed my eyes to give my mind a rest. A few minutes later, the phone rang.

I glanced at the caller ID and picked it up. "Hi Josh."

"Digger! You sound terrible," he bellowed in his exuberant telephone voice.

"Thanks. I feel lousy."

"You get hit on the head again?"

"No. Just thinking. Has the same effect. Why do you ask?"

He ignored my question. "Have you got time to come downtown?"

"Sure, why?"

"The boys at ballistics have found something interesting."

I found it funny that Josh always called lab techs and other such highly trained professionals "boys," even elderly women. It evoked an image in my mind of a bunch of six-year-old kids in oversized lab coats tinkering around and breaking expensive equipment before nap time.

"Can't you tell me over the phone?" I groaned.

"No. Meet me at the lab," he insisted.

"Okay. I'll be there in an hour."

"An hour? It's ten-thirty in the morning, Digger! What the hell are you doing that will take that long?"

"Power nap."

I detected a snort as he rang off.

After a shower and a change into presentable clothes, I revved up the old SMS—well, to be honest, it took a couple of tries to get the engine to turn over, and a few more before it would catch—and soon found myself purring down the 110 at a cool ten miles per hour. A short time and one micromance later—an older bottle blonde in a silver Range Rover—I passed the cause of the slowdown: a truckload of bananas had jackknifed across one of the southbound lanes. I tried to think of a good joke, but then had to concentrate to merge on to I-5.

Traffic broke up after that and I could go anywhere from twenty-five to eighty miles per hour in the bumper-to-bumper mélange. For good measure, a rusty haze hung over downtown like a filthy boa on a poor widow.

I met Josh outside a solid concrete building squatting between a glass high-rise and a porn shop just a few blocks from the sub-station. Josh took off his sunglasses, blinked at the haze a few times, and then put them back on.

"They have got to do something about the smog problem," he said.

"Okay."

"Digger! We breathe this crap in constantly! It can't be good for us."

"It's not. But you didn't drag me down here to chat about the weather."

"I'm just trying to be civic-minded like."

"That's big of you," I replied, as we stepped inside.

I couldn't see a thing after the glare outside, so after removing my own sunglasses, I just followed Josh's broad shoulders down a corridor to the left.

"To protect and serve," he said, barking a laugh.

A few minutes later, we came to a door marked *Ballistics*. Josh opened it and entered. I followed him into the cool darkness.

Now I really couldn't see anything. In fact, I bumped into Josh—"Watch out, Digger!"—before I realized we were in a sort of short hallway, an ante-chamber to the ballistics lab. Josh shut the first door and opened another door that led to a large, dimly-lit room with no overhead lighting at all. Rather, pools of lamplight illuminated microscopes and other squat, solid pieces of equipment. Between these pools, only shadows. I wondered how the folks who worked here managed to get around without bumping into things.

I bumped into Josh again, who merely grunted. Then he said, "Digger, I'd like you to meet Kujami."

"Kujami?" I whispered in the dark, seeing no one. "What kind of a name is that?"

"Shhh! Don't be rude. What kind of a name is Sharma?"

"Well, it was my father's name."

"There you go."

"No, I mean, is it his first or last name?"

"I never thought to ask."

A reedy voice echoed from the darkness. "It is neither first nor last. I am simply Kujami."

We walked toward the voice, but I still couldn't see anyone. One of the shadows, which I had mistaken for an enormous lamp, moved. Maybe unfolded is actually a better description. The man who stood and turned toward us reminded me of a fire-ladder opening up to reach a high window. Tall and thin.

He paused, muttering, "I'm sorry about the light," and reached with an impossibly long arm to turn on some dim fluorescents.

Even with the lights on I couldn't see him very well. When my eyes finally adjusted I gasped aloud at one of the strangest people I'd ever seen. Thick-rimmed glasses magnified his eyes, and he held his hands in front of him like a praying mantis.

"Kujami, this is Digger Sharma. Dr. Digger Sharma. Digger, Kujami."

"Delighted," murmured Kujami as I reached out to shake a hand extended from one of those impossibly long arms. "Welcome. And to what do I owe the felicity of this visit, inspector?"

Josh ignored my raised eyebrows. "Digger here's working on the Noakes-Blake case. I thought he might be intrigued by what you discovered."

"Ah, excellent. Are you a reading man, Dr. Sharma?"

"What? Well, a little, I suppose."

Kujami shook his head. "'Tis a shame, Dr. Sharma. For only in fiction can truth be told. Only in books can we roam the multitudinous conundrums of existence that otherwise must needs remain occult. Only in the liminal shadows can we caper at the summit and feast at the table of the sublime. It is not for the *dégagé*."

"Er . . . I guess," I replied, lamely.

"Oh, no need to guess. It is the very stamp of veracity. The imprimatur of verisimilitude, if you will." After a pause, he added "I myself am a writer."

"Really? How interesting." I tried to keep an edge of boredom from my voice.

"Mm-hmm. Beyond interesting, in fact. I am in the process of rewriting the classics."

"Rewriting them? I'm not sure I understand."

"Correcting them, revising them, updating them. For our modern times. You see, every epoch has its zeitgeist."

"Can't argue with you there." True. I had no idea what he was talking about.

"Indeed. My first project is to remove all references to gender and underlying stereotypes."

"So the characters are now all hermaphrodites?"

"Very witty," said Kujami, without the slightest trace of a smile. "My first project is Death of a Salesperson, originally by Arthur Miller."

I vaguely remembered a play I'd been forced to read in high school called *Death of a Salesman*. The main character Willie. Willie something. "So Willie...um..."

"Indeed. Willie Lohman is now Wilhelmina Layperson. Changes the story significantly, no?"

I gave Josh a look meant to ask, "Do we need to put this guy into a rubber room?"

He ignored me and said, "Kujami is one of our brightest, most talented forensic scientists."

Kujami bowed.

"However," Josh continued, "I'm sorry to push you, but we're in a bit of a hurry."

"Of course," he replied stiffly, bowing to me again. "Please excuse my digression. I thank you for indulging me."

"Not at all," I demurred.

He then led us over to a microscope. "Please sit and observe the object beneath the lens. Please be careful not to step on Kumado though."

"Oh, okay," I said, peering under the desk for a dog or cat. I saw nothing.

"Kumado is my friend. He is an arachnid, a spider."

I shuddered, picturing a huge, hairy, monstrous beast with nasty pincers.

"Never fear, Dr. Sharma. Even in life, Kumado was not dangerous, and he is even less so in death. Just be sure you don't tread on him."

Another look beneath the desk revealed a small body on its back, with many legs curled up over its belly. I couldn't stop myself from asking, "You keep a dead spider under your desk?"

"He was a good and loyal friend. I've known him almost as long as I've known Griselda here." He patted another microscope fondly.

I could think of nothing to say. I was about to run for the door when the reassuring but firm hand of Josh on my shoulder forced me to sit down. I blinked at a computer monitor, attached by a large-bore cable to a large black box.

At first, I could see nothing. Too blurry. Gradually, as Kujami made some adjustments, the image resolved into a kind of grayish ravine, sort of like what you see when you're flying into LAX. We zoomed through the luminescent canyon at a dizzying speed. The image was so captivating and realistic that, when we slammed into the rim, I almost jumped.

Josh laughed and even Kujami smiled. At least I think it was a smile.

"Dr. Sharma, you seem startled by the clarity and detail of the bullet."

"Bullet?"

"Look again."

I did. And then, I gasped, as I realized the degree of magnification.

"But how?"

Kujami smiled again—I think. "You are a man of science, Dr. Sharma, no? I thought it might amuse you to look through a scanning electron microscope."

I moved back to look at the monitor and computer.

"What you are seeing is a simulation, Dr. Sharma. The bullet is actually in here," he patted a large box about the size of a microwave oven with a half-dozen dials. Another thick, black cord snaked from the box to the computer.

"I'm impressed." I hated to admit it but I love a cool setup.

"We've been using electron microscopy in forensics for many years, but this one is fairly new. The resolution is to one one-thousandth of a micron, which is itself a millionth of a millimeter. It's called nanotechnology."

I whistled. "So this is how you examine a bullet nowadays?"

Kujami nodded. "And it's how we tell what gun has fired it. Please," he gestured toward the monitor again.

I peered at it again and soon found myself traveling along the canyon once more, this time slowly, with Kujami driving from the large box. He pressed a button on the side of the box and two strips of green numbers appeared on the top and sides of the image, rapidly flashing by as he moved us along.

"So you know where you are," I said.

"Correct. Also useful for bookmarking . . ." He pressed another button. This time, a small blue X appeared at a spot on the canyon and then drifted out of view as we moved along. ". . . or tracing," he added, pressing a different button.

A red line appeared, running along the side of the canyon, following the dips, curves, crevices, and peaks as it moved along, leaving an elegant tracing.

"So you can trace the shape?"

"Yes. But more than that. We can trace its *unique* shape."

"You mean like a fingerprint?"

"Precisely. No two gun barrels are identical, thus the bullet coming out of one specific barrel will leave etchings unlike any other."

"But won't each bullet fired change the barrel itself?"

"To some degree you are correct. I'm impressed, Dr. Sharma. But the variations are usually minor. We can program our software to correct for such variations, but for the most part, the etchings on bullets fired from the same gun will be almost identical."

"Identifying them unequivocally," I guessed.

"Exactly. And perhaps more important, legally." He paused, allowing me to revel in the tiny world of bullet etchings. "Now let's see what we have for comparison."

He turned a dial on the large box, and I peered at the red tracing. "This is a bullet fired from whose gun?" he looked at Josh.

"Blake's. Eddie Blake's," Josh replied.

"Yes, Mr. Blake's revolver. Observe the particular shape of the tracing, Dr. Sharma, along with its location."

I did so, thinking of the gun I had found in Blake's house. Kujami continued as he turned the dial. "This, conversely, is the bullet removed from the unfortunate Mr. Noakes."

Although the image changed and there were some slight differences between this image and the first one, they were essentially the same.

"Now, superimposed," Kujami said.

The two tracings appeared, one blue, one red. For the most part, they overlapped perfectly, forming a single, violet tracing.

"What do you conclude from this?" Kujami asked.

"It's the first bullet you showed me, the one you fired from Blake's gun for comparison, along with the second bullet, the one that killed Noakes. I would, therefore, conclude they were fired from the same gun."

"Really? That red tracing is of the first bullet you observed?"

I looked carefully but could see no difference.

"Yes, I'm sure."

"Very well. Let us again superimpose the tracing of the bullet that killed Mr. Noakes."

The two tracings appeared, mostly overlapping to form one violet line. When I looked more carefully, I noticed some differences from the first.

"It looks a little different from before," I said.

"Very good. Now here is a superimposition of all of them."

The violet line appeared with some patches of blue and red, but a third line of yellow also appeared. There wasn't much yellow because the lines overlapped almost exactly.

"So there are three different bullets here, not two!" I exclaimed.

"Precisely," Kujami said, gratified.

"Where did you get the third bullet?" I asked. "It looks like it was fired from the same gun."

"Indeed, Dr. Sharma. What you are seeing in the yellow tracing is a third bullet fired from Mr. Blake's gun."

"So where did you find this third bullet?"

"In Mr. Blake's temple. This bullet killed him. Fired from a distance. Not self-inflicted."

"Someone shot and killed him with his own gun?" I found this incredible.

"So it would appear. And there is the culprit."

He pointed to an object resting on a cloth on one of the countertops. It was the Smith & Wesson .38 I had found in Eddie Blake's bedroom.

I turned to look at Josh. He was grinning like the Cheshire Cat.

CHAPTER 23

OKAY, SOME LOOSE ends.

Someone killed Noakes with Blake's gun, probably Blake, but then someone killed Blake with his own gun. From what Kujami told us, it didn't seem possible that Blake shot himself. And since his body was found 300 miles from his gun, which was hidden under a pillow, we could pretty much rule out suicide. I thought back to those evil moments in the closet at Blake's place when Hawkface and Deep and Sonorous searched the house. What had Hawkface said? We did what we came to do. I now knew he meant hiding the gun.

So who *had* killed Blake? I had some hunches, but nothing firm to go on. Maybe Sloan. He tried to hire Blake to kill Noakes, it seemed. But then why kill Blake? To avoid witnesses? Possible, I guess.

And what about Jimmy the Snake? He seemed connected to Noakes. Maybe he even liked the guy. No. That would be too far-fetched even for Jimmy. But he might have been annoyed enough with Blake to have him killed.

Finally, Hawkface and his fellow goon, Deep and Sonorous. If anyone in their small circle had done in Blake, probably one of those two acting on orders from Jimmy the Snake. But from what I'd seen and what Josh had told me, Jimmy was small time. Why would he draw the kind of attention to himself that murder most foul invariably brings?

None of it made much sense. Sloan and Jimmy the Snake were somehow connected. But how? And if so, why had Jimmy or one of his boys tried to kill

Carmen? Maybe she knew too much. Maybe as a warning to Sloan.

Maybe because she had hired me.

No answers jumped out at me. I decided the key must be Carmen. I knew she had held back on me. And I had a feeling I'd end up like Noakes and Blake if I didn't figure it out. Also I wanted to see her again. My detachment seemed to be melting away. She had been discharged from the hospital a few days before so I called her up and told her I was coming over. Pushy but I didn't know what else to do.

When I got to the house, I felt a sense of déjà vu. The feeling grew stronger when I knocked and no one answered. Fighting down panic, I cut around the side of the house. Then I remembered the hired help had Wednesdays off and relaxed a bit. At least no rumbling sounds came from the garage but tension nagged at me. I skirted around the side yard once again expecting something to jump out at me.

Out back, I saw something that stopped me dead in my tracks.

Carmen was sunbathing topless next to the enormous, shimmering, aquamarine swimming pool. At that moment she seemed the most desirable woman in the world. My mind ground to a halt the same time as my feet. I don't know what was more blinding, her beauty or the light reflecting off the pool. Even though I wore sunglasses she still dazzled me.

Behind her stood an easel with a partially completed painting. Her palette and several brushes lay next to the easel on a chair. On a glass table covered by an umbrella lay a semi-automatic. The one Sloan had gotten for her.

She heard me. Sitting up in her lounge chair, she eyed me evenly for a moment, then picked up the top of her two-piece bikini, red with Hawaiian flowers and started to put it on. But then she tossed it aside, covering herself instead with a diaphanous cashmere and silk wrap of pink plumier that concealed nothing. It made her even more alluring. She wore sunglasses so I couldn't read her expression. She covered herself a little too deliberately for a woman surprised while nude sunbathing.

So I guess I was supposed to notice them. How could I not? Carmen's breasts, though not large, made up for in shapeliness what they lacked in size. From the generous splashes of cocoa brown in the centers, to the lighter olive that curved away in gentle slopes, you couldn't have improved them. Even with the wrap on, their outline burned onto my retinas like an afterimage.

"Hello Digger," she murmured.

I stood there for a good half a minute blinking stupidly, grateful for my sunglasses. They hid eyes that were bugging out of the sockets. Had it been a mistake to come over to see her again?

A smart detective would have turned around and left with steely resolve and stayed away until his brain returned to its regularly scheduled programming. But I had to get to the bottom of things and figured I had steely enough resolve to do it without getting into too much trouble. I owed it to Josh and Eddie and even Noakes. I knew Carmen had the answers so I had to be the tough guy.

I walked over and sat down across from her on a deck chair and smiled. "Hi Carmen."

She smiled back. "Digger. I like that name. Makes it sound like you've got a lot of energy."

For what? I wondered. *Whaddaya think?* answered the remaining few of my brain cells not bathed in a misty cloud of lust.

Now what?

Carmen lay down again, closing her eyes. Her wrap slipped off and slid to the ground. She didn't bother to retrieve it. "What kind of name is that?" she asked. "You said you were part-Indian. Is it an Indian name?"

"No. Ha, ha! Far from it."

I had to look away from her. Her tawny skin reflected more sunlight than I would have thought possible. I had a sudden urge to jump on top of her and kiss every part of her body, from her jet-black hair with blonde highlights, slicked back and cascading over her shoulders, to her petite toes, in all their maroon-polished perfection. Instead, I studied a hydrangea bush in all its pink perfection.

"My mother told me she named me after a basketball coach," I replied. "A coach from the University of Notre Dame. I guess she was watching the game just before she gave birth." I looked back at Carmen.

"Watching a basketball game while she was in labor?" Carmen cocked her head, the idea incredible to her, even more so than the origin of the name itself.

"Well, pregnant women sometimes get these crazy urges you know. Like cravings for ice cream or pickles or—"

"It's not just pregnant women who get crazy urges Digger," she said, playfully poking me with one of her perfectly tanned, perfectly manicured feet.

As I had told Josh, an ethical detective doesn't sleep with his clients. It blurs the boundaries. You miss things. You do stupid things. You get in trouble. Keeping your distance is the right thing to do and I desperately wanted to do the right thing. But I didn't know how to respond so I did nothing.

After a minute or two she stopped poking, sat up, and leaned toward me with a pout. "Why did you come here, Digger? Just to tell me about your family origins?" She ran her tongue across her upper lip.

Disappointing. If a woman is trying to seduce me the least she can do is show some class. Not that a lack of class had ever stopped me before but a guy's gotta have some standards. She lay back down again.

"No. My family doesn't interest me," I answered.

"Why not? They seem so romantic."

"Romantic? What's romantic about a guy knocking up his girlfriend and then skipping town? A strange idea of romance."

She turned and sat up facing me once again. I couldn't take my eyes off her. This time she removed her sunglasses and gazed at me with her brown eyes. "What's strange about it?"

Then she leaned over—we were only a foot or so apart—and kissed me.

Yes, on the lips.

CHAPTER 24

THIS MIGHT BE a good time to pause and tell you a little more about myself. You already know about my family and that I practiced medicine until a few years ago when my license got suspended but you don't know the rest. I'll fill you in because it's kind of important for you to understand a few things to better appreciate how I felt with Carmen's lips pressed to mine.

I had been a doctor. And not just any old doctor but a psychiatrist. Yeah, a shrink, a bug doc, a p-doc in good parts of L.A., a quacker in bad parts of L.A. And less flattering terms.

I had a great life. One of those "silk-stocking" or "boutique" practices in Brentwood. You know, the kind where the worried well who have given up on religion come to you for absolution. A certain lifestyle goes along with that type of work. A nice home, nice cars, a trophy wife. You name it I had it. I kept only my car, the trusty SMS, from my time in med school and residency. For some reason I couldn't part with it, even though my wife hated it. Ah, my wife. A kind, sweet, patient, beautiful woman, but not particularly intellectual. I realized a few years into our marriage I found her dull. I still loved her in some abstract way but found myself increasingly absorbed in my practice for mental stimulation.

There are, of course, pitfalls in relying on work for everything. For example, a lot of patients—female patients—who, well, let's just say they had some deficits in the judgment department about men they dated. They didn't find the excitement or even basic human companionship they craved with those men. Some of them understood, eventually, that they had unrealistic expectations. That no one could live up to their ideals. That no one can be interesting all the time. That all guys who didn't measure up weren't jerks. But most of my female patients never reached that level of understanding. So you can guess who they turned to for comfort.

And I like to think I did comfort them. But I had my limits. There were certain things I would not do. Certain places I refused to go with them.

But one patient was different.

Alice.

It would be nice to be able to say I remember when I first met her. But I can't. Plain by most standards, she had been a patient for some time before I really noticed her. She had a pile of dark hair, a pleasant face, although with too much makeup, and a smile that made you feel like you had at least one friend in the world. Her eyes: what color were they? Funny, I can't remember. At any rate she had a matching set that always seemed to be gazing fondly into mine.

Again, it would be great to be able to say when she and I noticed feeling an unusual connection but my memory is hazy. What I do remember is that I started looking forward to her sessions. Then I let our time go beyond the hour. Then we got together outside of therapy. You know, coffee, chatting, that sort of thing. We called each other by our first names. Though not strictly unethical these sorts of things blur boundaries, ones a smart shrink avoids crossing.

Her intelligence made it seem okay. Incredibly bright, her intellect appealed beyond any sort of physical attraction. I do remember that I did not, in fact, find her beautiful.

I made up all sorts of excuses in my mind to rationalize our peculiar relationship. My wife would understand if she knew but oddly I never got around to telling her. Husbands and wives keep some confidences from each other that don't damage the marriage but would be so difficult to explain that they remain secrets.

We got into the habit of emailing. Like our coffee and lunches our messages remained a secret. They were never anything more than playful, usually focused on books or articles we had read. But they were discussions about ideas, something sorely lacking in almost every other part of my life. Not dangerous. Or so I thought.

Our therapy sessions remained separate from this other secret life. We always maintained a strictly business-like atmosphere in therapy. She talked about her problems. I listened. In between sessions the lunches and emails continued.

Then one day Alice arrived for her session strangely agitated. Prim and proper as usual but fidgety, opening and closing her purse, refusing to make eye contact, and generally out of sorts. After some of the usual check-in questions she turned to me with an odd expression, her lips pursed, her eyes bright and excited.

"Digger! Remember when you said therapy can change people so they aren't so unhappy."

I nodded, unsure what direction she was taking.

"And you told me a good way to change is through a new experience."

"Yes. And by a new experience," I explained, sensing an unidentified danger, "I meant a new experience of a relationship. So for someone who feels stupid, I listen to their ideas with respect and interest. For someone who feels put down, I say things to encourage them and build them up. And for people who use bad behavior to get attention, I try not to get mad when they are being provocative so they can experience someone not getting angry. That's what I meant."

Alice sat quietly for a long time. She looked up at me a few times and then looked away. Finally, without a word, she stood up, walked over, and kissed me.

Yes, on the lips.

That moment I remember. As I didn't find Alice physically attractive, the idea of an earthy connection had never crossed my mind. In that instant, though, I realized clearly it had occurred to her. Stunned, I did nothing.

When I didn't kiss her back she drew away and gave me the strangest expression, a look mixed with affection, fear, anger, and disappointment, her head cocked to one side. After studying me intently for a moment she exhaled and silently turned away, picked up her purse, and left my office.

She unnerved me so much that I cancelled the rest of my afternoon patients and went for a bicycle ride, something I find soothing. Unfortunately, I couldn't stop thinking about Alice. I worried about repercussions. Doctors are strongly advised not to get romantically involved with patients. The code of ethics forbids psychiatrists from getting involved with theirs under any circumstances. I hadn't really done anything wrong.

Or had I?

I never encouraged Alice to think of us as having a romantic connection. At least I didn't think I had. Even though we met up outside of sessions and exchanged emails, my behavior had been above reproach, or so I thought. But as I pedaled along the L.A. river, it dawned on me I had missed something, something so obvious I should have spotted it the first time I met her. But my affection for her blinded me to it. The revelation so startled me that I stopped and parked my bike against a fence, just staring out over the smog of Los Angeles. Stared at it without really seeing it, sweat running down my face.

Alice had borderline personality disorder. Uh oh.

I ticked off the list of diagnostic criteria for this disorder, one of the most difficult to treat. The most prominent symptom? Instability. Unstable relationships, an unstable sense of self and other people, even an unstable sense of reality. The term itself referred to the borderline between psychosis and neurosis. The diagnosis could be treated only with difficulty but never cured. If you've ever seen the movie *Fatal Attraction*, the Glenn Close character was a borderline. Same with Winona Ryder's character in *Girl, Interrupted*. And a lot of men wrote songs about crazy borderline women: "Cecilia" by Simon & Garfunkel, "Rhiannon" by Fleetwood Mac, "Runaround Sue" by Dion, "Mustang Sally" by Wilson Pickett, even Caroline in the song "Pretty in Pink" by The Psychedelic Furs.

Alice had all the classic symptoms. Fear of abandonment. Unstable relationships. An unstable ego. Impulsivity. Self-destructive behavior. Poor judgment. Lack of trust. Drug addiction. Promiscuity, even by L.A. standards. Extreme emotional swings. Explosive anger. Chronic feelings of emptiness.

History of childhood sexual abuse. She checked all the boxes.

I slapped myself on the forehead. How could I have been so stupid, so blind? A terrible thought occurred to me. What if she made a complaint to the Medical Board? One of the worst things that could happen to a physician apart from being sued.

The infamous Board went after doctors with a zeal not seen since the Spanish Inquisition. Usually for improper bookkeeping or billing. Sometimes for bad prescribing practices. Sometimes for drug or alcohol addiction. But all doctors knew illicit relationships with patients were the worst. The Board always came down most heavily on those offenders.

I licked my lips but found my mouth dry. Still gazing out across the city, I drank some water from my bottle, unable to see the hills lurking in the smog. This was bad. Borderlines do not let things go. They are incredibly destructive, in both their own lives and those of everyone around them. I knew that hoping for Alice just to let this drop was naïve. She had told me about things she had done, vindictive things against men who had wronged her. I couldn't help feeling that she left my office numbering me as one of them.

As it turned out, she accused me of sexual harassment. Even though I had never had any such complaints against me before, the patient advocate nominated by the Board to investigate the case had a crusader's mentality, considering all doctors accused of misconduct guilty until proven innocent, with a stated of intention "weeding out the bad apples." My words in my own defense fell upon deaf ears.

All the things that followed—my wife's feelings of betrayal, the email messages, which Alice produced as evidence, my fruitless attempts to defend myself, my divorce, and losing my house and pretty much everything else, including the three-year suspension of my license to practice medicine— seemed like something in a movie, things happening to another person.

But that moment I remembered: her lips pressed to mine.

As Carmen's lips were pressed to mine right now.

CHAPTER 25

I OPENED MY eyes and tried to read Carmen's expression. Eyes closed, she wore a dreamy look. I cupped her face in my hands and gently pushed her away. "No."

She opened her eyes. "What?"

"No. I can't do this." I took off my sunglasses.

"Do what?" She batted her eyes at me.

Surprised, I burst out laughing. Who bats their eyelashes nowadays? "I can't get involved with you this way Carmen. You hired me to, well, I don't know why you hired me, actually. But I can't sleep with you. I may not be a good detective but I'm an ethical one. I can't."

"Can't or won't?" Her eyes narrowed in anger.

"Both," I said.

She looked away and gnawed at her bottom lip. "Maybe you just don't understand." And she kissed me again. With her tongue this time. She then pushed me back onto the deck chair and straddled me, kissing with all her might. She had ashtray breath. My resistance wavering, I struggled weakly.

"Señora!" The sound startled both of us.

I opened my eyes to find Miss Gulch gaping at us wide-eyed, hands covering her mouth. Standing up too fast, I not only knocked over Carmen but tripped over my chair and ended up flat on my back on the lawn. From this undignified position I heard Carmen shout several words in Spanish. I couldn't understand them, but her tone was unmistakable. Ominous, furious, threatening, terrible.

As I struggled to my feet I saw Miss Gulch turn pale and back away, stumbling over a chair, and then turn to run back into the house. Carmen stood up and put on her bikini top.

"I thought Wednesday was her day off." I tried to keep my voice level as my heart pounded.

"It is," Carmen said, her jaw clenched.

"So?" I asked.

"What?"

"So whadda we do now?"

"That's not funny," she snapped.

"You're right. It's not funny," I growled. "And you know what else isn't funny? Two men are dead. They might not have been good men. They were not ethical men that's for sure. But they were human beings. Them dying is very not funny.

"And you know what else isn't funny?" I continued, letting my anger boil over. "You hiring me and then lying to me about everything! You didn't hire me to find out if Lamont was having an affair. You knew he wasn't cheating on you! So why did you hire me? I don't know. But I'm getting fed up with bullshit and being strung along!" I walked up close and confronted her. "Carmen, do you really need my help?"

She bit her lip and looked away.

I decided to bitch-slap her if she started crying.

Instead, to my surprise, she bitch-slapped me. "Bastard!" she spat. And ran into the house.

I stood rooted to the spot, stunned, my cheek stinging. How could she do this when I was being noble and ethical for a change? It hurt too, dammit. I hate getting slapped.

I turned to study the painting on the easel. It depicted a man. No one I recognized, but clearly a man. Like the one hanging in the living room, she had executed this painting in the Cubist style, with multiple perspectives and geometric forms, the man fractured into different parts. A head here, a leg there, a face from different angles. But with one common theme.

Violence.

Guns, knives, spears, instruments of torture—you name it. Every single body part shot, stabbed, mutilated, mangled, or crushed in the most horrible ways imaginable. I sat down, unable to take my eyes from the awful scene.

I then thought about Carmen, going back over all of my interactions with her and all of her behavior. And a terrible thought struck me. Carmen Sloan had borderline personality disorder. Just like Alice.

Oh no.

CHAPTER 26

ALTHOUGH NOW CONVINCED that Carmen held the key to solving both cases, I felt it reasonable to assume she would not be cooperative. Maybe it was time to talk to Lamont Sloan and reveal my true identity. You know, like a super-hero. But he probably already knew all that.

I called Josh to ask him to request a background check on both of the Sloans from "the boys at the bureau."

"Why? What happened?" he asked.

"I got kissed and then slapped."

"By who?"

"Carmen Sloan."

"You kissed her?"

"No, she kissed me. I didn't kiss back."

"And her husband slapped you?"

"No, she did. I got kissed and slapped by the same person."

He tried stifling his laughter but some muffled snorts escaped. "That seems harsh."

"It was harsh. I hate getting slapped."

"You're not used to it by now?"

"Very funny."

"Sorry," he demurred.

I then told him what I wanted to do.

"I don't think it's a good idea to confront Sloan," he said.

"That's an argument for doing it," I replied.

"You kill me Digger!" He snorted as he hung up.

This time when I called Sloan's office I had no problem getting an appointment. Nothing like saving a guy's wife's life for getting you shoehorned into his busy schedule.

After seeing his house I expected Sloan's office to be just as fancy. So I got a pleasant surprise when Lamont's Angel escorted me into a plain, sparsely furnished room. No doubt the simple wood paneling and floors cost a few bucks. And his desk, though elegant, took up little space. Soft cornflower-yellow leather covered all the chairs along with a low sofa.

Sloan wore an elegant but simple Oxford shirt with blue pinstripes, charcoal slacks, a paisley tie, and maroon braces. He sported rimless glasses that I hadn't noticed in the hospital. He also wore an expression of polite curiosity.

"Please sit down Mr. Sharma," he invited, directing me to a chair. "Thank you again for everything. I hate to think what would have happened if you hadn't come along when you did. Most fortuitous." He passed his hand over his face and then ran his fingers through his hair, dark with some graying at the temples. "May I offer you a drink?"

I nodded. "Just water please."

He stood to cross the room to a small wet bar. He fixed himself a scotch with ice and handed me a glass of water.

Thirsty from the heat, I downed it gratefully, the crystal glass heavy in my hand.

"Now then," he continued, "how may I help you Mr. Sharma?"

I peered at him over my glass. "The question, Mr. Sloan, is how can I help you?"

He arched an eyebrow. "I'm not sure I understand," he replied. "You said you worked for one of the clothing shops on Rodeo Drive. I usually get my suits tailored by Dolce & Gabbana."

"So Carmen hasn't told you?"

He frowned. "Told me what?"

"That I'm not really in the fashion biz. That I'm a private eye. And that she hired me."

His eyes widened, his surprise genuine.. "She . . . she what? You? Oh." He looked away and stared out the window at the honking cars, the pedestrians stopping to chat, before turning back to me. "Okay. Well, that explains a lot. So that's why you were out at the house."

I nodded

"Goddammit all," he grunted. He downed his drink, stood, and poured himself another, staring out the window, again distracted by the traffic on Wiltshire Boulevard. He then turned on me, eyes blazing, his voice rising in anger. "Why did she hire you? And what is it you want? Money? Are you trying to blackmail me too?"

"Please, Mr. Sloan. I'm not your enemy. And I don't want your money." Man this guy was touchy. "Someone tried to blackmail you?" Without waiting for an answer I continued, "I think you're in danger. I'm convinced Carmen is too. And now that I think about it, so am I."

He turned to look at me. Then he nodded and sat down again, composing himself with several deep breaths. He then spread his hands wide, palm open, inviting me to continue.

"Mr. Sloan, your wife hired me about a month ago. She told me she thought you were having an affair."

He snorted.

"I now know you're not. And I think she knew that from the start. So I don't know why she hired me. But since then, two men have been killed, I've almost been killed twice, and Carmen has also almost been killed. To get to the point, you need to tell me what the hell is going on."

Sloan sighed, nodded, and drained his second scotch in one pull. "I know how you feel." He went to the bar for a refill. I wondered if he always drank so much before lunchtime. Maybe he understood the stakes better than I did. He turned back toward me.

Standing, I decided to press my advantage. "What do you know, Mr. Sloan? I don't know if I can help you and Carmen, but I can't do anything unless you tell me what's going on. You've got to be straight with me, otherwise you risk us all getting killed." He stared at me, his expression unreadable. Then he looked away and sipped his scotch.

"Look! I don't know if you did something illegal and I don't care," I pressed on recklessly, exasperated by his insouciance. "But you're in some kind of trouble. That's why people hire private eyes. To get them out of trouble when they can't go to the police and they can't solve their problems themselves."

Sloan looked down at his glass and then at the decanter in his other hand. Instead of pouring himself another drink he set them both down with a solid clink. He then stared at me, his expression as cold, hard, and unyielding as the granite bar.

"Please at least try to trust me." I pleaded. "I think you're involved in something that's spinning out of control and you don't know what to do." It was a shot in the dark, but I thought I might be on the right track. His answer surprised me.

"Who are you doing this for?" he asked quietly.

"What?"

"Are you doing this for me? For yourself? For Carmen?" He eyed me steadily. "Don't think I don't know what kind of woman she is." Sloan smiled for the first time, but without humor. "You'll be a lucky man, indeed, Mr. Sharma, if you can go through life and avoid falling into the clutches of a woman like her."

I was stunned. This was no way for a successful Beverly Hills attorney to talk about his trophy wife. Clearly, I had wildly underestimated and misunderstood both Sloan and Carmen. I decided to risk one more shot in the dark. "Carmen told me about your past. Does that have something to do with what's going on?"

To my surprise, an expression of indescribable sadness passed across his face.

"My past?" he repeated, talking to himself. "My past." He paused, looking down at the carpet. "Okay, Mr. Sharma. What did Carmen tell you about my past?" He sat down on one of the buttercream chairs and motioned for me to do the same.

I relayed as much as I could remember.

He remained silent for a long time after I finished, several minutes, during which he ran his fingers through his hair. After a hint of a smile, he nodded his head a few times and looked at me. "Mr. Sharma, I am very grateful for all you have done for me. And Carmen," he added. "But the truth is, I have nothing in my past of which to be ashamed, irrespective of what my wife has told you." An angry gleam flashed in his eyes. "So," he rubbed his hands together and stood, "there is nothing more for us to discuss."

I stood as well. "Thank you for seeing me. But I think you're making a mistake, Mr. Sloan."

"Am I?" He shrugged as he shook my hand. "You don't know all you think you know." He held the door for me. As I walked out, he added, "A mistake, Mr. Sharma? A mistake? I don't think so. Far from it in fact." And he closed his office door.

CHAPTER 27

THAT EVENING, OVER a candlelight dinner at a famous—that is to say, expensive—restaurant, I relayed to Belle all the details of my meetings with both Sloan and Carmen. After stealing a lovely, matched crystal salt and pepper shaker set, she tapped her teeth with her nail.

"I don't believe either of them," she finally said.

"I don't either."

"This woman"—that's what she had taken to calling Carmen Sloan—"she is much smarter than you think. And I think she's playing you."

"I'm sure you're right. But why?"

She shrugged. "I don't know. Are you sure you don't know her? An ex-girlfriend, maybe?"

I shook my head. "I'm sure I would remember her."

Belle smiled.

"And not for that reason!" I laughed. "There's just something compelling about her. And that's not necessarily a good thing."

Belle spread her hands. "*Novio*, a woman like that is used to playing with men like this . . ." And she wrapped her napkin slowly around her little finger.

"Yeah," I sighed. "It's probably second nature to her now."

She nodded. "But her husband. I think you should go with your stomach on him."

"You mean my gut?" I smiled.

"Yes, your gut! There's something about him that makes me think he's dangerous and ruthless. I would stay out of his path."

"And the wife?"

"Stay out of her path too."

I nodded. "Good advice."

We enjoyed a lovely meal and conversation, and I screwed my courage to the sticking point to tell Belle that I really loved her when she surprised me by saying, "I have some sad news for you, *novio*."

Rarely serious, she made me worry something might be wrong with her. "You're not sick, are you? Your family okay?"

"Oh, *novio*!" she laughed. "You're a good person to ask. I'm okay. They're okay."

"But?"

"But I have some news that will make you sad."

I silently squared my shoulders and braced myself. The low clinking of glasses and silverware and the murmur of conversations surrounded us, servers darting silently back and forth in the dim lighting. Classical music played in the background

"I'm going to marry Antonio," she said, in a quiet voice.

"Antonio?" Who? I didn't know any Antonio.

"Yes, he's a professor of particle physics. We met at the symposium on black holes."

I felt myself slipping into a black hole of my own. I mean, I always knew Belle had other boyfriends and that she might marry one of them. But in a theoretical kind of way. And anticipating something doesn't prepare you for it. My indecision and hesitation made me lose Belle. "But . . ." I protested weakly.

"No buts, *novio*. I like you a lot, but the other day Antonio confessed he loved me."

"But I had planned to tell you I loved you!" I exclaimed.

Taken aback, she sat up straight. "Why didn't you?"

"I guess I didn't get around to it."

She raised an eyebrow.

"In time, that is," I finished, lamely.

She took my hand. "I'm sorry, *novio*. I didn't think I would ever want to remarry. I like my freedom too much."

I smiled, wryly. "I guess this Antonio must really be something!"

She thought about it. "Actually, not really. But he told me we could marry and I could still have my freedom. I'm not sure you could abide by such an arrangement."

I thought about it. I'm not the jealous type. But an open marriage wouldn't be my style, either. I felt sad but not devastated. "Yes, you're probably right." I thought about it. "Do you really think you'll be happy?"

She nodded.

"Then you have my blessing!"

"Oh, *novio*! Thank you for taking it so well."

She paused, looking at me sideways.

"What?" I asked.

"It's just that . . ." She looked up at me, her eyes glistening. Belle did not cry easily or often. In fact, I had never seen her cry before. "Would you come to the wedding?" she asked.

"Of course," I laughed. "I'd love to!"

She squeezed my hand again while her eyes squeezed out tears of joy. "Thank you, *novio*."

Later, when I dropped her off at her house, I felt a pang of sadness in knowing that, even if I came to visit her here again, it wouldn't be the same. Still, what can you do?

She hugged me at the door for quite a long time and then kissed me on the cheek before going inside. I started back to the car with a heavy heart and gazed into the sad evening. No stars. It wore the black of mourning. I moved to wipe away a tear.

Only then did I realized my pocket handkerchief was gone.

CHAPTER 28

"DIGGER, I THINK you need a vacation," Josh observed in between bites of a hot pastrami sandwich. We ate lunch at a deli on Colorado Avenue in Old Town Pasadena. A bright, fairly clear day by L.A. standards. You could see the hills through the windows. Traffic noise rushed in whenever someone opened the front door, vanishing as it closed.

I had just related to Josh my encounter with Sloan.

I munched thoughtfully on my Reuben for a moment. After swallowing, I replied to his observation. "Oh? Do I look that bad?"

"No!" he laughed. "You look fine. I thought maybe you should get out of town for a few days, though." His eyebrows did the samba thing and he even winked.

Obviously up to something. I decided to play along to find out what. "Any idea of where I should go or—even better—how to pay for this vacation?"

"San Francisco. Ah, yes! The city in the fog by the bay! Cable cars and crab cakes."

"I thought crab cakes came from Maryland?"

"Really?" He frowned. "Well, whatever. Scratch the crab cakes. But think of San Fran. The gateway to the orient! The Golden Gate Bridge, the scenic vistas, the—"

"Traffic and congestion? Don't forget those."

"Oh, yeah. You lived there for a while, right? Well, my point is, SF would be a great place to get away from all this," he gestured vaguely toward the soda fountain. "Give you a chance to relax, recuperate."

"Okay, Josh, I'll bite. Since it's obvious you want me to go to San Francisco, maybe you could just tell me why."

He smiled. "A bit obvious, perhaps?"

"You have all the subtlety of a nagging wife," I replied.

He frowned.

"Okay, that's a bit harsh," I quickly demurred. "But why San Francisco?"

"Digger, there's a woman who lives there I think you should meet."

I groaned. "This can't be about setting me up with some girl."

"No, no, no," he shook his whole body to emphasize his point. "This woman might prove valuable to us in a, let's say, mutual investigation."

I lowered my voice. "Does this have something to do with Eddie?"

He growled, "Yes," and ground his teeth.

I said nothing but just munched on my sandwich.

He continued. "This woman's name is Dawn. Dawn Coeur-Lyons."

I raised an eyebrow. "You're kidding?"

"Yeah, I know, it's a hoot. I think it's a pseudonym."

"Ya think?"

"Shut up," he suggested. "But get this. She is, or was, Alfie Noakes's old girlfriend."

I shrugged. "So what? What would she know that could help us?"

"Lemme finish. She was Noakes's squeeze. That is, until she left him for another guy she met through Noakes —"

"Lemme guess, Frank Sinatra?"

"Haw! That's good! You're an idiot, Digger. No, Jimmy Alveoli, well known to you and me as Jimmy 'The Snake.'"

I whistled. "Okay, you got my attention. So she lives in San Francisco?"

He nodded.

"Well, why don't you just call her up?"

"Uh-uh. Wouldn't work at all. See, she hates cops—"

"I like her already."

"Very funny. Shut up and listen. She hates cops and wouldn't give me the time of day. Hell, wouldn't piss on me if I was on fire." He laughed again. "No, it's gotta be someone she won't be suspicious of from the start. You're the guy for the job."

"Okay, let's say I do this, let's say I talk to her. Why do I have to go up to the Bay Area? And for that matter, how can I afford it?"

"Me and the boys will pay your way." His jaw tightened and his face became hard again. "We feel it's the least we can do for Eddie."

"Okay, I'm convinced. But—"

"I'm getting there, Digger. What's the matter with you, attention deficit disorder? We want you to go up there, because this Dawn, well, I don't think she'll just talk to you over the phone."

"Why not?"

"She's a prostitute."

"Oh." I thought about this. I could use a vacation. "Okay."

CHAPTER 29

TWO DAYS LATER I found myself on a plane bound for SFO. Josh, good to his word, had arranged for my flight and a hotel in The City. I agreed to cover incidentals. I brought a book—my Franklin Library selection, *Cry the Beloved Country*—and a three-pack of condoms. Those were sort of to bolster my confidence. I'd never been to see a prostitute before and didn't know if they provided their own rubbers. Of course, I didn't want to ask Josh.

"Well, maybe prostitute's not the right word," Josh had said when he dropped me off at the airport. "More of a high-class escort."

"Terrific."

"Don't worry Digger! We've got you covered."

"So what's the plan? I call her up for a date and then pump her for information on Jimmy the Snake and Alfie Noakes?"

"Ha ha! You kill me Digger. But, yeah, something like that. Anyway, we've already set up an appointment for you with her."

"Appointment?"

"Yeah, that's what they call it."

He showed me her picture.

I whistled. "Fine. I still think this is a bad idea."

"It's okay. We know a doctor up there. He checked her out to make sure she didn't have VD or something."

"Thanks. That's very reassuring. Explain to me again why you can't go up there yourself?"

"I'm a cop, Digger! She'd smell that a mile away. Besides, I have a reputa-tion to uphold, you know. To protect and serve."

"Oh, thanks. And I don't?"

"That's me, Digger. A lonely beacon of self-restraint . . ."

"You're not listening," I said.

". . . the last bastion of defense between the respectable citizens of this great if smoggy city and the rough hand of crime . . ."

"Uh-huh."

". . . a respected pillar of the community."

"Shut up," I suggested.

His laughter rang in my ears.

We touched down at SFO in the early evening, giving me time for a shower, shave, nap, and dinner before meeting with Dawn. I'd had a strange and short conversation with her to confirm my appointment, like I was going to see the dentist. She confirmed our "rendezvous"—her term, not mine—in a polite, professional way.

Clearly, I needed to learn to speak French.

We scheduled to meet at 9:00 at an address on 31st Street off of Lin-coln Avenue in the Sunset District, just south of Golden Gate Park. My seedy downtown hotel off Market Street nestled between a massage parlor and a parking garage. I made a mental note to kill Josh the first chance I got.

After freshening up, I flopped on the bed and pulled out my notepad with questions I'd scribbled down on the plane. Some from me, others from Josh. I scanned the list to see if we'd forgotten anything important.

He wanted me to get answers to his questions and any follow-up ones without letting on that I knew anyone involved, or that I was a PI working on the case, or that I'd been bankrolled by the heat. I couldn't think of any clever way to do all this, so I decided to wing it.

In other words, it seemed hopeless.

But Josh had insisted. We might get something—anything. Even one lead might be all we needed. And if I couldn't get her to talk, well, at least I'd get laid. I made another mental note to not just kill Josh but to do so in a slow and painful way.

I had six questions:

1. Nature of relationship with Alfie Noakes?

2. Nature of relationship with Jimmy the Snake?

3. What kind of people are they?

4. What are they involved in?

5. Seen either of them lately?

6. Why prostitution?

I had contributed the last question. Why do we always want to understand people?

Maybe to understand ourselves.

Who the hell knows?

I had some time to kill, so I pondered something that I hadn't given much thought to before now—the moment of truth, as it were. It went against my ethics to sleep with clients. It also went against my ethics to sleep with prostitutes. But I had accepted Josh's offer. Why?

Although unclear to me why my moral compass wavered in this instance, I had some shadowy ideas. Given the illicit nature of the sex trade in most of the United States—save for the forward-looking state of Nevada—it's obvious most men cannot resist the lure of the forbidden. More than the moth to the flame, we are drawn to hookers and brothels by their very illegality. Perhaps thumbing our noses at authority and daring them to stop us gratifies our sense of independence. In the 20s, moralistic temperance leagues failed to foresee that prohibition would give rise to organized crime with its far-reaching effects. Now, the hypocritical guardians of righteousness failed to realize that by criminalizing prostitution, they elevated it. They opened the door to illegal sex-trafficking to meet demand, placed the escorts in grave danger, and forced the cops to waste their time pursuing "vice" while real crime flourished.

But what can you expect of a country that thinks sex is worse than death?

At any rate, it made me smile to think that the cops had set this up for me.

At 8:30, I called for a taxi and gave the address to the driver. As we drove through the city up Geary Street, a light rain began to fall. The other cars seemed to hover above the glistening road, gliding on runners of pure light.

My heart hammered unpleasantly in my chest as I pondered what awaited me.

CHAPTER 30

THERE'S NOT A lot I remember about that evening with Dawn, although I recall being surprised by her appearance. For some reason, I imagined a woman with the name Coeur-Lyons—alias or not—would be young and French and look like Brigit Bardot.

Not even close.

She answered the door barefoot. A mass of curly black hair encircled her angelic face. Her tight black jeans and black T-shirt looked like they had been painted on. Maybe they were. They barely contained her full-figured Eurolatina figure like a bomb about to explode. About thirty-five years old I guessed.

For some reason, she felt it important to tell me her background. I guess we all want to be understood. Brazilian born of Italian ancestry, an exotic combination. She had light olive skin, full, ruby lips that curled up at the corners as if laughing, large, brown eyes, high cheekbones, and freckles. Needless to say, I completely forgot about Carmen Sloan and pretty much every other woman I had ever met. I guess that's the point—and the reason for the expense.

Her lovemaking, extraordinary. I'd never been with a prostitute before and so didn't know what to expect. Even the word escort doesn't seem to do justice to her level of expertise. Clearly in the right line of work, amazing, although hard to explain how or why. She just seemed to know all the right things to say and do, the right expressions to make. I do have one lingering image that, well, the best description, from my perspective, the ace of spades in a deck of cards.

I'll leave it at that. Yet, there was something too detached about her for it to be truly erotic. Strange. Lots of red candles dimly lit her apartment, the scent of incense wafting through. Mysterious and oddly shaped hangings covered the walls, as if trying to lull me into another reality. Pillows everywhere. But the effect was contrived, forced.

Anyway, when my brain returned, I started making small talk, mostly out of nervousness. I couldn't help noticing that she had nipple rings with diamond studs, so I asked about them.

She glanced at them with mild interest and said, "Oh, these? A gift from an admirer."

"Well, I'm not surprised. That you have admirers, that is. I bet most guys who meet you fall in love with you."

"That's so sweet!" she said and kissed me. Soft ambient music played quietly around us.

"Did he get them for, um, there?" I asked, pointing at her breasts.

She laughed. "No! They're earrings. I like them better here." She toyed with them absently. "Still, diamonds . . . a girl's best friend." She looked sad for a moment. Then she perked up. "I like 'em. Can't eat diamonds, though." She opened a drawer on the nightstand and pulled out a granola bar. "Snack time! Do you mind?" I smiled and she pulled out another for me. We munched on our bars together in a companionable silence.

"I do like diamonds, but they look better here, don't you think?" She asked, wiping crumbs from her lips.

I nodded, my mouth full of granola.

"Makes me feel different from other girls."

She didn't have to explain what she meant.

"And this too," She toyed with a labial ring. "It's a bit exorbitant, but, as you said, I've got admirers who provide for me."

I turned to stare at her. "You seem well educated."

She laughed again, this time with a trace of bitterness. "You mean for an escort?"

"No! I mean, yes . . . I mean, um, you're not at all what I expected."

"Oh? What did you expect?"

"*Hmmm.* You're well-educated, intelligent, and, well, elegant."

"So you're saying I'm not good at what I do?"

"No! Far from it. You're very good at your profession."

She nodded in agreement.

"I'm sorry, I'm not saying this well," I said.

"That's okay. I think I know what you're getting at. You're wondering why a smart, attractive, elegant woman like me is doing a job like this."

I nodded.

She leaned over and kissed me again. "You're very sweet. In fact, I could say the same thing about you. You're not my typical clientele."

"Oh? What do you mean?"

"Well, you're obviously a professional. I would guess a doctor."

"Wow! How on earth did you know that?"

"You're very sure handed. You also know where to touch a woman to make her feel good."

I blushed but doubt she noticed.

"And you've never been with a 'woman of the night' before."

I laughed. "A woman of the night?"

She laughed too. "Yes, it does sound a bit tawdry, if romantic. At any rate, you've never done this before, have you?"

"That obvious?"

"From your pillow talk. Most guys don't like to talk afterwards."

"Do you mind?"

"Not at all. It's a refreshing change."

"Okay. Do you mind if I ask you another question?"

She shook her head.

"Do any of your admirers get jealous?"

"Oh, Digger. You haven't fallen in love with me, have you?"

"Er, perhaps. I'm not sure yet."

She smiled. "Well, yes, they do get jealous. But that's their problem not mine."

"What about boyfriends?"

"Yes, they get jealous too. That's why I have so much jewelry. They think they can buy me. But the joke's on them. My body might be for sale, but I'm not." Her eyes flashed in a way that surprised me.

I didn't know what to say, so I stroked her hair for a moment. She sighed.

"So what is it about diamonds that girls like so much?" I asked.

She shrugged. "I dunno. Boys like 'em too."

"Did the boy who gave you these"—I nodded toward her breasts, thinking of Eddie's enormous gemstone—"like diamonds?"

She looked at me askance. "That's an odd question. Why do you ask?"

"No reason. Just wondering."

She then looked away for a moment, glancing around her bedroom as if trying to memorize it, then said, "Yes, he likes diamonds. Nothing wrong with that. He's not like all those boy zeroes you meet who don't have a fucking clue."

"Boy zeroes?"

"Yeah, you know the type. Those losers who think that if they take you to dinner at a high-class place they're gonna get into your pants. And then, if they do, they're too proud to consider you and what you might want."

"I'm sorry. Sounds like you meet a lot of those. My gender is a constant source of embarrassment to me."

"Many of them are. But don't worry. You're not. You're sweet." She kissed me again.

I could get used to that. "I'm beginning to see how other guys fall in love with you."

She laughed and pushed me away. Then she kissed me hard.

A few minutes later, I tried a gamble. "Is his name Jimmy?"

She started and pulled back. "How did you know?"

"Lucky guess. You've got that name tattooed on the back of your shoulder. Here." I gently touched it. A rattlesnake coiled around the name.

She shivered. Then she relaxed and turned her head to look at it. "Yeah, I forgot about that."

"Does he treat you well?"

She turned to face me. "Does it matter?"

"Guess not."

She sighed and looked at the clock. "You'd better go."

"Okay."

"You take care, honey." She kissed me one last time.

"Thanks. You too." We got out of bed and I dressed.

"And don't worry about me. Diamond Jim treats me just fine. In fact, he's gonna take me away from my sordid life." She fished a gorgeous engagement ring from the drawer of the night stand. "See?"

Even in the poor light, the massive and beautifully set stone glittered like hope. Jimmy must be a generous guy. Heck, if I could afford a ring like that to take her away from her sordid life, I would be a generous guy too.

"Did he say when he'd take you away?" I joked.

She cocked her head. "Yeah, in fact he did. Next week. Said something about his ship coming in."

I smiled.

She smiled back and kissed me at the door. Sweet.

We liked each other but knew we'd never see each other again. More than a micromance but with the same effect.

Sad how life goes sometimes.

CHAPTER 31

I HAD MY book, *Cry the Beloved Country*, to amuse me and relieve some of the boredom on the flight home. Still thinking about Dawn, I opened it up and started to read. Although my mind wandered, I followed the story pretty well.

For some reason, a few paragraphs into Chapter 3, something caught my attention. I didn't know at first just what. Merely a sense of something very important in the words. A description of a man, a man who lives in the countryside, visiting a large city. Important. I reread the passage several times, wondering why.

It actually reminded me of an experience many years ago, when traveling in Great Britain. For reasons I can't recall, I found myself in the city of York and decided to go see the famous York Minster. I walked from my B&B toward the cathedral, shrouded in mist. Even if it had not been foggy, I would not have seen it until I was almost on top of it because the path leading there follows narrow city streets with high walls. And then, all at once, I found myself in a large courtyard. Through the veil of mist, the cathedral loomed, impossibly large, imposing, and magnificent. The most amazing thing I had ever seen. I'm sure that a good part of that amazement—maybe the best part—arose from not having seen it at a distance before seeing it close up. I guess that's how we experience the best things in life.

With the same sense of momentous discovery, I realized what had captured my attention in the book. A single word: *lorry*. I read it over and over and then said it aloud, finally grasping what it meant: a British word for *truck*. *Lorry*. But aloud, it sounded like a name—*Laurie, Lori,* or even *Lorre*. Funny how English works. One sound, many meanings.

I couldn't stop staring at it. After my sudden recognition of what that word meant, several other words from Blake's answering machine fell into place. Together with what Dawn had told me, I realized I finally had the last piece to the puzzle.

I guess I'm not such a boy zero after all.

CHAPTER 32

"THE PORT OF Los Angeles is America's busiest port with a 7,500-acre harbor." So said the website. It went on to acknowledge the port's world-class facilities as a "one-stop shopping concept of cargo transportation and delivery favored by most shipping lines." A modern port interconnected with train and truck networks.

The website also shared just about every detail of every ship that entered the port, along with its cargo. It's a matter of public record, there for the taking. I looked up the registries of all ships scheduled to dock in the next week to find which one might connect with Jimmy the Snake. At first, I made the mistake of searching only for ships registered in Belgium. Then I realized most ships are not registered in their country of origin. So I changed the search and found three ships due to call in L.A. that had sailed from Antwerp.

I ignored two cruise ships and focused on the third: the *Peder Skram,* a bulk carrier Danish-built by *A/S Dampskibsselskabet Torm*. She left Antwerp about two weeks ago and was due to arrive in L.A. on Monday. Two days from now.

I called Josh.

"Damn! You must be the greatest detective since Oliver Wendell Holmes," Josh said.

"I think you mean Sherlock Holmes."

"Whatever. Brilliant, Digger! Just brilliant!"

Wednesday. Forty-eight hours after the *Peder Skram* docked. We drove through thick smog north on Highway 2 to the Sloan place. Our plan: to make an arrest. Josh had stopped by my digs and said I deserved to be in on the action.

I jumped at the chance to go and told him the Sloan staff had Wednesdays off.

"Even better," he growled.

A lovely evening unfolded over a surprisingly mild and clear early summer day, slowly embrowning the meanest city in America and turning into a gorgeous red and pink sunset. For some reason the smog didn't seem too bad. Or maybe it enhanced the sunset.

"So whaddidja find?" I asked.

"Oh, all kinds of crap. The usual contraband. No big deal. Although the shipping company had kittens!" Josh laughed. "But we also found the gemstones. Both cut and uncut diamonds. Worth a fortune. They estimated the take at between $60 and $70 million. Jesus! Can you believe it?"

"Yes," I replied quietly.

"Anyway, the bastards hid those diamonds amazingly well. Took us forever to find them."

"Where were they?"

He laughed. "So damned clever I'm surprised we found it at all. They shipped about a ton of tulip bulbs on ice. They hid the diamonds in with the ice in a refrigerated container."

"And diamonds in ice look like ice." Clever indeed.

"Yup. We never would have found them, not in a million years. Even then, we needed a bit of luck. One of the officers, a guy named Scherzer, knew that tulips come from Holland, not Belgium, and that raised his suspicion."

"So how did you find them then?" I asked.

"We ran a check on the shipment. You know, sender, receiver, buyer, seller, all that stuff. And, whaddaya know? The seller turned out to be a Belgian shell company, well known to Interpol. The Bureau then got involved. They seized the shipment. But not before they congratulated us on a job well done."

"That's all?" I felt a letdown.

"Well, that, and the receiving company. A subsidiary wholly owned and operated by White River Industries."

"Who are?"

"Who are owned by none other than our friend, Jimmy the Snake. The FBI guys said he's used the company for smuggling before, although they never could catch him. They learned about it through one of their informants."

"*Ahhh.*" Now I felt satisfied.

"Yeah. Officer Scherzer noticed some water, you know, from the melted ice. He saw that some of the ice had melted, but the rest hadn't. Well, that didn't make any sense, of course, so he took a closer look and, bam! There they were."

I sat back, sighed, and reflected, agreeing with Josh. A job well done.

After a moment, he asked, "But how does that book fit in to all this? How on earth could you have found something in a book written—what, over fifty years ago? —that would help you unravel all of this?"

"The word *lorry* gave it away."

"Huh? You lost me around that last turn, Digger."

"*Lorry* is a Briticism for *truck*. Once it dawned on me, I realized we had misunderstood the whole message."

"What message?"

"The one on Eddie's answering machine from Noakes."

"Oh?" He furrowed his brow, puzzled.

"Yeah. Noakes was talking about two things and a person, not two persons and a time."

"I don't understand."

"Well, when we heard the words—or at least what we thought were the words—*Laurie, Jim,* and *dawn,* we assumed that the first two were names and the last a time of day, dawn. What he actually said, in his excited Scottish brogue he apparently never lost, was *lorry, gem,* and *Dawn.*"

I pronounced the word *gem* to rhyme with *hem,* not with the British pronunciation, which did sound more like *Jim.*

"So you see, his message referred to a lorry—a truck—that was going to pick up the gems you guys found. The reference to Dawn? Dawn Coeur-Lyons, girlfriend of Jimmy the Snake, high-class escort. And, I suppose we now know, gangster's moll."

After a suitable pause, Josh asked, "How'd that go, by the way—with Dawn?"

"Great. Thanks."

"Don't wanna talk about it?" he prodded.

"No." I said firmly, brooking no parley.

"Oh, c'mon, I deserve some vicarious pleasure!"

I laughed.

Josh shook his head. "Anyway, amazing. But what made you think it was diamonds coming in? How did you know they were on a ship that docked today?"

"Something Dawn said helped me realize when and how the shipment was coming in."

"Oh yeah?"

"She said Jimmy told her he would take her away from her sordid life—as he termed it—this week, because his ship was coming in. She didn't realize he was speaking literally instead of figuratively. She wore expensive earrings and showed me the impressive engagement ring Jimmy the Snake had given her. I had suspected diamonds were at the bottom of this ever since we found that rock at Eddie's place. The one that Norman Gatz connected with the heist three months ago at the Antwerp Diamond Centre."

"Fair enough."

"As for that gem, I wonder if Sloan gave it to Eddie as his piece of the pie."

Josh shrugged. "We'll probably never know."

I shrugged in return. "You're probably right. As for sending it via ship versus, oh, I dunno, air freight, I did some guesswork. What Jimmy the Snake had told Dawn about his ship coming in helped, of course. But also, Gatz told me the haul must be quite large and bulky. I figured the authorities were closely watching all the airports and roads out of Belgium for a shipment that big. So I guessed they would ship it. There's a lot more places to hide stuff on a ship than an airplane or a truck, and they usually aren't as well searched for practical reasons."

"You're right about that," Josh replied. "The boys at the dock search maybe one out of twenty of those containers. And even then, it's just a quick and dirty job. There's no way we would have found the diamonds if you hadn't pretty much told us what to look for."

"Exactly. As for when, I just searched the schedule for ships arriving this week from Antwerp. I figured it had to come from Belgium because the heist had taken place there and the gang hadn't been able to smuggle their haul out of the country. In fact, I bet they kept the stash hidden somewhere in Antwerp the whole time. After all, they had a lot of stuff and probably figured no one would actually look for it in the city. You know, the old wisdom about hiding something in plain sight. As for the ship, the *Peder Skram* was the only cargo ship from Antwerp due in for the next week, so I made another lucky guess based on what Dawn said."

Josh whistled. "Amazing."

"Something else Dawn said to me that made me realize it was the diamonds. She called Jimmy 'Diamond Jim,' a moniker we hadn't heard before, and she told me he had given her the diamonds she wore. I'll bet her engagement ring was also part of the Antwerp heist. It got me thinking maybe this whole thing revolved around smuggling the rest of the diamonds into the US I mean, Sloan might be rich, but not that rich. And Jimmy the Snake? As you said, small time. Maybe he thought he could muscle his way into something bigger. Something that would make him fabulously wealthy. Anyway, Sloan somehow got a line on the operation and wanted a cut."

"Oh, he'll get his cut all right. He's gonna spend the rest of his life at Pelican Bay if I have anything to say about it," growled Josh through clenched teeth.

"Pelican Bay?"

"It's a prison up north."

"Oh. Why a life sentence? I mean, I know this operation was a major crime, but that seems pretty stiff."

"Don't forget Eddie and Noakes," Josh reminded me. "Sloan's an accessory to one murder and might have masterminded another."

"Ah." I remained silent for a few minutes out of respect for the dead. I knew it was eating away at Josh too, so I let him ruminate a bit before asking, "So what did you find out?"

He shook his head as if to clear out the cobwebs. "Well, like you, I'm pretty much going on hunches but I think I'm right. We've definitely linked the shipment to Jimmy the Snake. The boys from the Bureau are going to take care of him up in the Bay Area. In fact, I wouldn't be surprised if he's already in custody. I don't think his goons had a chance to warn him because the FBI kept their operation very hush hush. The freighter truck they sent to pick up the shipment hadn't arrived when I left. But they caught a nasty character with gold teeth—"

"Hawkface," I interjected.

"What?"

"That's what I called him. He met with Sloan. I figured him to be one of Jimmy's men."

"Oh, yeah. Well, you're right about that. His name's Fisher. Anyway, they took him into custody right off the bat."

"Did he put up a fight?" I asked.

"Not really."

That surprised me, but I didn't say so. "So that takes care of Jimmy the Snake."

"Yeah," he replied. "As for Sloan, like I said, I think we've got enough to pin a case on him. Most likely, we'll get him for smuggling along with a dozen INS violations, obstruction of justice—you know. The usual."

"What about Noakes and Blake?"

Josh set his jaw and glared at the traffic, which slowed us down on our way out to the Sloans. Even with the gridlock, we'd be there in ten minutes. "As I said, I think he helped plan both murders, but it's going to be hard connecting either to Sloan," Josh growled.

I nodded. It was going to be hard to pin anything on Sloan unless Jimmy the Snake, Hawkface, or one of the others squealed. Circumstantial evidence. I don't know if there's any honor among thieves, but none of the guys involved were very honorable. Based on the drawing I had made in my kitchen and what Josh was telling me, the seed of an idea started to germinate about how everyone might be connected.

Josh interrupted my reverie. "I'm sure as hell gonna *try* and nail Sloan, though. Bastard," he spat. "Unless you've got any ideas."

"Well . . ." I hesitated to tell him what I was formulating, as I hadn't had a chance yet to think it all through.

"C'mon, out with it!" he prodded.

"Well, pure speculation, but I think I know what the relationships were."

"Oh yeah?"

"Yeah. Remember the old movie, *Strangers on a Train*? A Hitchcock film, I think."

Josh shook his head.

"It doesn't matter. What matters is the plot. Two complete strangers meet on a train. They strike up a conversation and both learn the other has someone in his life he wants to get rid of."

"Uh huh. Go on."

"So they make a pact. One agrees to kill the other guy's wife so he can marry his mistress; while the other agrees to kill the first guy's mother so he can inherit the family fortune."

After a moment, he exclaimed, "No motive!"

"Bingo. If complete strangers kill both people, there's no motive. No obvious one, anyway. And without a motive, it's pretty hard to solve the murders."

"You got that right." Josh tapped the steering wheel, thinking.

"So that's what I think happened," I continued. "Blake put the bite on Jimmy the Snake and Noakes blackmailed Sloan. Jimmy and Sloan put their heads together and came up with a plan. Jimmy and his guys would get rid of Noakes if Sloan got rid of Eddie, providing each other with alibis without apparent motives. That's why Sloan went up to the Bay Area about a month ago, to take care of Blake. And why Jimmy lured me out to the docks a few weeks ago. That way, Noakes and Blake would be discovered at a time when both Sloan and Jimmy had alibis. That's why they didn't kill me. I was their witness."

"Yes! That explains it!" Josh banged on the steering wheel twice.

"They used the same gun, as we know," I concluded. "A mistake because it connected the two murders. But they didn't think anyone knew about the link between Noakes and Blake, so no one would try to match up the bullets."

"Yeah, the gun you found had been fired recently. The boys in the lab were sure of it. They couldn't tell how many shots, of course, and the cylinder was empty. Jimmy's boys must have done that before putting it back in Eddie's house, figuring no one would make the association."

"Makes sense. My guess is that they never imagined someone would figure out which gun killed either of them or that they were in any way related. We got lucky because we knew about their relationship."

"More than luck, Digger." He turned to smile at me and then continued. "What about that connection? How do you think Sloan ever got mixed up with someone like Jimmy the Snake?"

"Again, speculation," I said. "But my guess is that the link was Noakes."

"Noakes? Why Noakes?"

"Sloan defended him once on a case."

"Ah. I didn't know that."

"Yeah. I expect Sloan somehow found out about the diamond scheme but didn't want to get his hands dirty. Noakes was probably the most dangerous and therefore the most reliable criminal he knew, so he recruited him. From there, Noakes likely introduced him to Jimmy and that's how the whole operation got started."

"And then Eddie and Noakes got greedy."

"Yeah, that's probably it."

Josh leaned back with a satisfied expression. He floored the accelerator. "Let's go haul in that son-of-a-bitch."

CHAPTER 33

WHEN WE PULLED up in front of 30279 Beverly Glen Road, I had that old feeling that made the hairs on the back of my neck stand up. And not just because of what seemed to happen every time I ended up there. You know—insulted, gassed, and worst of all, slapped.

This time because of something else, an impending dread that came over me as we pulled up and saw a black Cadillac coupe parked in the drive. I glanced at Josh, and he shook his head. Before we got out of the car, he called for backup. "But kill the sirens," he added. He also had them run the plates on the Caddy.

Within seconds, we learned that the car had been registered by White River Industries—the receiving company owned by Jimmy the Snake.

Touché.

"No point in getting in over our heads. I like at least even odds," Josh said.

"How can odds be even?" I wondered.

"Shut up, Digger."

We got out of the car and looked around. No one in the coupe, which struck me as odd. You'd figure a guy like Jimmy would want someone to cover his back. Then I realized everyone else had been arrested. We thought Jimmy had been arrested as well.

I guess we were wrong.

We scanned the front of the house but saw nothing. A low murmur came from inside the house, possibly a television set. As I rounded the car, listening hard, a muffled bang startled me, followed by a scream.

Josh pulled me to the ground behind the coupe and lay prone himself.

A few seconds later, another muffled bang.

After a tense moment, during which we heard nothing more, Josh turned to me. "Stay here." He got up and half-ran, half-crept to the front door, whispering urgently into his mobile phone.

Ignoring his instructions I got up and followed him.

He tried the door. Locked.

He saw me and frowned, but then, with a resigned expression, motioned to me to get back and drew his semi-automatic from its shoulder holster.

We listened again for a moment. We heard a faint noise, but I couldn't identify it.

In one swift motion, Josh aimed at the deadbolt and shot it several times.

Another scream came from inside the house.

Holding out his hand to keep me behind him, Josh kicked in the door and followed his gun inside, which he held out in front of him with both hands. Turning this way and that, he looked around in the entrance hall and then motioned for me to follow him.

We heard a woman wailing like a wounded beast.

Josh looked at me and raised his eyebrows.

I shrugged but feared for Carmen. What had happened to her?

The wails came from the second floor so we cautiously made our way up the carpeted stairs to the landing, where a grisly sight greeted us.

Blood everywhere. I've seen my share of blood, but I couldn't believe how much the two bodies had spurted out. The two dead bodies. A third body—Carmen—very much alive, lay draped across Sloan emitting a cry of sorrow like nothing I'd ever heard in my life.

I did the only thing I could think of to do. I fainted.

CHAPTER 34

WHEN I CAME to, I examined the other body which I assumed was Jimmy the Snake. Pretty clear they both were dead because Sloan had been shot through the head—many of his wonderful brains splattered on the wall behind him—and Jimmy through the chest, blasting most of his heart out of the window behind him.

Blood everywhere. On the walls, the windows, the ceiling, the carpet—two large and widening pools—and on Carmen.

I've never liked the sight of blood and I still felt nauseous and dizzy, but some doctorly instinct must have kicked in as I examined first Jimmy, then Sloan, to see if there was any hope.

Nope.

Both had pretty much bled out, Jimmy from his gaping chest wound, the bullet most likely severing his aorta, and Sloan from his head wound. Sloan's wound suggested Jimmy had nailed him right between the eyes.

Although not thinking especially clearly, a question nagged at me. Both wounds would have caused death instantaneously. But I had heard two shots fired several seconds apart. How could that be? I figured I could ask Josh to see if he had heard the same thing. Maybe I misremembered it, still a little woozy.

Sighing, I stood up and looked at Josh, his gun still at the ready, looking at me quizzically.

I shook my head. "Uh-uh."

He lowered his gun and holstered it, his hands shaking.

I went over to Carmen, who had by now subsided into quiet sobbing, and led her downstairs away from the carnage.

A few minutes later, a couple of L.A.'s finest joined us, radioing for the forensic team. Fifteen minutes later, the CSI guys arrived to begin the thankless task of cleaning up the mess. Josh and I sat quietly with Carmen around the coffee table in the living room. She had cleaned up a bit, but blood still streaked her hair. Someone wrapped a blanket around her. She shivered and stared blankly at the floor, apparently in shock. Three other police officers joined us.

"I know you're probably not doing too well right now Mrs. Sloan," said Josh, soothingly, "but do you think you could give us a brief account of what happened?"

She nodded, eyes still on the floor, sniffed a few times, and then pulled herself together. "Can I have a drink?" she asked.

"Sure. I'll get you one," Josh replied. He poured her a generous scotch on ice from the sideboard, handed it to her, and pulled out a notepad. One of the other officers also pulled out a pad to jot down her statement.

"Could I have a cigarette too?"

I got up and fished her gold-plated cigarette case from her purse, which she had set on an end tablet. I found a lighter and handed them to her. Absently, she lit a cigarette and took a couple deep drags. "I just . . . I don't know what to say."

"Well, just tell us as much as you can remember," Josh prompted. "Maybe we can start from before it all happened. When did your husband get home?"

"About an hour ago. He got back from the office about 5:00."

"How was he acting?"

"He seemed, I don't know, worried, preoccupied. He didn't say much, and I kept having to repeat things to him. We were supposed to meet with some friends tonight for dinner, and I had to keep reminding him . . . you know. That kind of thing." She paused. "I guess I should call them and tell them we're not coming." She started crying again, burying her head in her hands.

Josh and I looked at each other.

After a moment, Josh said, "Mrs. Sloan, I don't think you need to worry about that. We'll take care of it." He motioned to one of the other officers, who nodded, obtained the necessary information, and left the room.

"Can you go on?" he asked.

She nodded and looked up again with mascara streaking from her tears. She unconsciously wiped it away. "So about, I dunno, maybe twenty minutes ago, the doorbell rang. I was in our bedroom"—she pointed vaguely upstairs—"getting ready to go, and Lamont called out that he would get it." She turned to Josh. "Today's the maid's day off, so there was no one else home to answer the door."

He nodded.

"So next thing I know, there's this yelling and shouting coming from downstairs. I ran out on the landing up there," she pointed again, "and I saw Lamont and the other man down here. I didn't know him. I'd never seen him before."

"That's okay. Go on," Josh said.

"Anyway, they were arguing, and Lamont looked up and shouted, 'Get back in the bedroom!' So I went back in the bedroom, and then heard more shouting and the sound of someone running up the stairs. Lamont, I think. Then I heard him go into his study. After a minute or two, the other guy came up the stairs. There was more yelling, then gunshots. I ran out and saw Lamont . . . ohhh!" She began sobbing again.

After a few minutes, she pulled herself together and downed the rest of her scotch. "It's so confusing. Lamont was lying on the floor, sort of holding his head and shouting. He was bleeding. The other man stood there pointing a gun at him. Lamont had his gun out too, pointed at the other man. Then Lamont shot the other man. The impact threw him back against the wall and he collapsed. One of the windows behind him was shot out. I don't remember much else. Only that Lamont . . ."

She stopped—a blank, lost look covering her face—and she looked down again.

Josh looked at me. "You think she's going into shock? I think we've got enough to go on."

I shook my head, holding out my hand for him to wait.

He looked surprised but nodded.

We sat in silence for a few minutes, but Carmen said nothing more, staring blankly at the floor. Finally, she stood, as if in a trance, and turned to leave.

I stood up as well. It was my turn. "All right Carmen," I said, none too gently. "How about you sit back down and let's tell everyone what really happened."

CHAPTER 35

CARMEN FROZE.

Josh froze.

Everyone froze.

It was like an Alaskan photo shoot. No polar bears, though.

Josh turned to stare at me with a shocked expression, clearly thinking I'd lost my mind. Out of my peripheral vision, I noticed the other two officers turn to look at me with curious but guarded expressions.

Carmen betrayed no emotion, staring at the floor. "What?" she said, trying and failing to inject confusion into her voice

"Digger," growled Josh in a low voice. "What the hell are you doing? She's in shock!"

"Oh? In shock? Really? I wonder."

She finally turned to face me.

"You have to have feelings to be in shock," I snapped. "Carmen has no feelings because she's a stone-cold psychopath. No emotions, no empathy. You've never been shocked at anything in your whole life, have you, Carmen?"

She flushed but stayed calm. "I don't know what you mean."

"Oh, I think you do."

She flushed again, this time with anger. "I don't know." She glared at me.

"You planned this, right from the beginning, didn't you?" I pressed.

Josh shook his head. "Digger! I'm warning you—"

I held up a hand. "Hold on a minute, Josh, let's see what Mrs. Sloan has to say for herself."

"I don't know what you mean, Digger," she pleaded, attempting to give her tone some warmth. "I never wanted any of this to happen!"

"Maybe not quite this way," I said, "but oh, yeah, you wanted this to happen. That's why you hired me in the first place."

"What?"

"It took me a while to figure it out, but I finally got it. You hired me to be your fall guy. You found out about the plans—your husband's and Jimmy's. You needed someone to do your dirty work. Someone whose ethics were already compromised and whose morals were, well, let's just say, a bit on the shady side. Or so you thought. You wanted someone to kill your husband and then take the rap. Either that or be killed by him, which would have accomplished much the same thing. I was gonna be your sucker."

"This is absurd! You can't talk to me like this!" she snapped.

"Ah, but I must. You knew about the diamond smuggling scheme. You wanted in on it. And I was your stooge. You hired me to pit Lamont and me against each other. How easy it would have been! The immoral lover? The jealous husband? No one would have questioned what happened. They certainly wouldn't think you had anything to do with it. Then you could turn in either Lamont or me with your hands clean and walk away with Lamont's share of the $80 million."

"You're insane," she whispered.

"Am I? I'm pretty sure you didn't plan what happened tonight, but it still worked out just fine, didn't it? I'm sure Lamont's got a nice big fat life insurance policy. It's not gonna be tens of millions, but it's probably quite a few, right? Maybe not a mansion in the Cayman Islands, but enough to keep you lounging on a beach somewhere warm and sunny for the rest of your life with handsome young cabana boys bringing you drinks with umbrellas. No matter what, you would get Lamont's share and come out smelling like a rose. Either way, you stood to make a fortune, Carmen, and you were the only one who couldn't be connected to it. Only I didn't go along with your plan."

She said nothing.

I looked at Josh.

He raised his eyebrows as if to ask, *Are you sure about this?*

I nodded.

He sighed. "Mrs. Sloan, you have the right to remain silent. Anything you say can and will be used against you in a court of law. You have the right to consult with an attorney and to have that person present during questioning."

Carmen's expression changed from confusion to anger to hatred and back a half dozen times. Finally, she settled on confusion. "I don't understand . . . am I being charged with something?"

"Dr. Sharma's making some pretty serious accusations, Mrs. Sloan, so yes, you are. Conspiracy to commit murder and fraud to start with. There may be others."

She looked at me, and all at once, an astonishing arrogance came over her. "You have no proof. You've got nothing on me! You're bluffing to try to make me, well, I don't know what, because I didn't do anything! You're a bastard and an asshole too! I'm grieving the loss of my husband, and you dare to accuse me of—"

"Cut the theatrics, Carmen. I've got all the proof I need."

That got her attention. She narrowed her eyes.

It caught Josh's attention too. "What do you mean?" he asked.

I stepped toward Carmen, but she held her ground. "You hired me because you thought I was tainted," I said. "You knew my license to practice medicine had been revoked, and you knew why. You figured you could hire me to do whatever you wanted because no one believes a fallen doc. You planned to seduce me and control me that way. If worse came to worst, I had no credibility. You probably figured I was corruptible. That was your first mistake."

"You can't prove a word of that."

"Oh? Well, let's see. We have proof that you hired me. I've given all the evidence of that to Lieutenant Cohen here."

Carmen glanced at Josh.

"You did try to seduce me. I've got no proof, true. It's your word against mine. But your maid did catch us out by the pool."

She shifted from one foot to the other, eyes darting around, but still said nothing.

"Next, you knew about my past."

"You can't prove that!" she shouted.

"Actually, I can. I got a letter from the California Medical Board a few weeks ago to notify me that someone had checked into my license. That puzzled me. Why would someone do that? I hadn't applied for a job.

"So I called the Board to see if I could find out who had made the inquiry and why. As you know, all information regarding my license is a matter of public record and available for anyone to see. Imagine my surprise in finding out that Eddie Blake had requested it, acting on behalf of someone at your address! At first, I assumed Lamont had asked him to do it, even though I couldn't figure out why. Then I realized Blake had done it for you."

Carmen snorted.

"I'm guessing that you had been looking around for private eyes who fit the profile you were looking for, someone with a questionable past. I can imagine there are quite a few of those in L.A. Who knows how many saps' records you sifted before, through sheer dumb luck or cunning, you somehow stumbled across me—a physician who'd had his license suspended. It's easy to find out why because that information is a matter of public record. But you were clever. You used Blake's name on the application to the Medical Board so no one could trace it to you. You must have been ecstatic when you read the report! It put my credibility in question. What a goldmine! Or so you thought. As I said, you needed a fall guy with a checkered past."

I paused and held my hands out in a gesture of resignation. "You found me, Carmen, because you were looking for someone like me."

Her eyes flashed with anger.

"Then you found a mutual acquaintance, Bernie, to make everything look legit."

"That's a lie!" she roared, balling her hands into fists.

I ignored her and continued. "I figured it would be pretty easy to check with Bernie. So I did. He had never mentioned me to you. You made that up. You thought I had no integrity because of the charges leveled against me that lost me my license. You were wrong. I never did those things. They found me guilty based on the accusations, in spite of my telling them they were lies. But I was innocent. I'm not the corruptible chump you thought I was."

She glared at me, hatred burning in her eyes.

"Your second mistake. You let on that you knew I'm a doctor. I wondered why you called me *doctor* instead of *mister* a few times, but I never said anything. The only way you could have known was through the Board. I guess you slipped when you called me that. I decided not to point it out to you."

She laughed sarcastically.

"Your third mistake. Planting that gas-soaked burning rag. Foolish and unnecessary, Carmen. Someone who wanted to kill you would have just drugged you and put you in the car with the motor running and the garage door closed. They wouldn't have put the rag in the tailpipe. I'm guessing the smoke was something you thought would make the whole scene more dramatic. Instead, it was a giveaway."

"I hate you." Her voice growled low and threatening.

"Mrs. Sloan? You don't have to answer any more questions," said Josh.

She waved him away impatiently, as if shooing an insect.

I smiled. Not too triumphantly, I hoped.

"You still can't prove anything," she snarled. "Okay, so what if I did look you up and hire you? There's nothing illegal about that! You can't connect me with, well, whatever it is you're saying I did."

"Actually, I can do that too. You see, you made one other mistake that is a matter of public record. I don't know why the police didn't talk to you about it. Maybe they didn't think it important at the time."

Josh stared at me. "Be careful, Digger."

I glanced at him. "Don't worry. It's nothing you guys would have thought about, really."

He stared at me with some hostility, as did the other two officers.

Carmen glared at me too, openly furious.

"The deadbolt," I said, simply.

Their looks all changed to confusion.

"The deadbolt on the garage. It was locked from inside the house."

The looks of confusion changed to mild curiosity.

I turned to Josh. "The day that Carmen claimed she was 'attacked'—her words—and locked in the garage with the motor running? She said someone tried to kill her. But she was lying."

I turned to her. "No one tried to kill you, Carmen. You made up the whole thing."

She stared daggers at me. "You're the one who's lying!"

"Oh? Then who bolted the garage door from the inside? That puzzled me for the longest time! How, I wondered, did the door to the garage get locked? It didn't make any sense for a person—a fictitious person, as we now know—to drag you to your car and then go back inside the house to lock the door to the garage! I mean, you could go out the other door or open the garage door. So I think you locked it from the inside earlier and forgot to unlock it before you went out to come in from the backyard. You set up the whole thing yourself."

No one spoke.

Carmen deflated. "Okay," she said. "You're right. I did set you up. But is that a crime? I did nothing against the law."

Josh and the others all relaxed.

"What about murdering your husband?" I asked.

"What?" said Josh and Carmen at the same time.

The other two officers stared at me, shocked.

"Yes, you shot him after he shot the other guy, didn't you? You figured only by killing him could you salvage something, with the original plan kaput. That whole thing of weeping over Lamont's body and everything else, all just an act, right? True, your husband had just shot Jimmy, but I suspect you were glad about that. One less thing for you to have to do."

"I loved my husband," was her pathetic reply.

"You hated your husband," I retorted. "And he hated you."

She stared at me, mouth open, clenching and unclenching her fists, body taut.

"I think you were expecting a share on the diamond scheme, which you knew about from the beginning. I don't know if you told Lamont you knew, but he found out."

"How?"

"Because I told him."

She started, her eyes wide, her hands balling into fists.

"When I told him you knew, he was clearly surprised. He probably told you to mind your own business. Or maybe he promised you a cut. At any rate, he was not happy. Then Jimmy found out. Before or today, I don't know. But when he learned that the ship had been searched and the diamonds impounded, he got royally pissed off and knew who to blame.

"My guess is that Jimmy came here today to confront your husband and tell him things had gone sideways. So you heard the scheme had gone south. Bad. You might be in danger. Then Lamont shot Jimmy. From the look of the wound, it would have killed him instantly.

"You ran from the bedroom—just as you said—and saw what happened. You had to think fast. You might be next. Then, you realized shooting Lamont with Jimmy's gun would be more or less the perfect crime. With Blake and Noakes and Lamont and Jimmy dead, there would be no witnesses. Nothing could tie you to the diamond smuggling scheme. And the police would assume the two men shot each other like in a Quentin Tarantino movie. You would get off scot-free. You would then receive a large insurance policy settlement and move to some tropical paradise to live a life of leisure."

No one moved. Everyone stared at Carmen, who wore a blank expression.

"You said they shot each other. That's impossible," I said.

She glared at me, eyes narrowed, fists clenched, jaw tight, body tensing as if to run.

"They'll find your prints on Jimmy's gun, Carmen. He was already dead when you aimed it at your husband. I can only imagine what he thought. Then you shot and killed him. Again, the wound would have been fatal and instantaneous. But Lieutenant Cohen and I distinctly heard two shots, several seconds apart. Neither of those men could have survived long enough to fire a second shot. You fired the second shot, killing your husband with the dead man's gun."

A complete and stunned silence throbbed.

"That's how it happened, isn't it?" I prodded her.

Without warning, Carmen leaped across the coffee table at me. Startled, I didn't have time to react. She slammed me against the loveseat and we both tumbled over the back of it. By the time I had scrambled to my feet, heart pounding, scratch marks on my face, Josh and the two able-bodied officers had restrained her.

Barely.

She screamed obscenities at the top of her lungs and wrestled like a wildcat. Even the three much larger men struggled to contain her. Eventually they had enough and rolled her over prone, cuffing her.

After five minutes or so, she stopped fighting and yelling. Breathing hard, she looked at me with a look of such pure hatred that I shivered and left the room.

Waiting in Josh's car, I saw them lead her out to one of the squad cars.

Before they loaded her in, she glared at me one last time.

Even almost insane with rage, even darting looks of such venom, she remained one of the most beautiful women I had ever seen.

CHAPTER 36

A FEW WEEKS later, Josh and I were sitting outside having lunch at a street café in Old Town Pasadena. I tried to wrap things up for Josh regarding Carmen. A pleasant hum of traffic underlay the low chatter of the other customers. A gorgeous sun beat down on us, making me glad we were under a red umbrella. Tourists passed in that uncertain way they always do.

". . . so she knew that Sloan wasn't having an affair. It was just a pretense to hire me. She wanted to use me as leverage against him."

"Why didn't she just divorce him if she hated him that much?" Josh asked.

"I dunno. I'm guessing she signed a prenup. She wouldn't have gotten much. I mean, she probably would have been comfortable, but nothing like what she would have gotten if the diamond heist had gone off. Then she could have demanded and gotten a fortune and just moved away. The best of both worlds. She gets what she wants—you know, gets away from Sloan with a whole lotta money. As it turns out, she still might have gotten the insurance payout."

"Yeah, that's true. We checked into it. The policy was for $10 million."

"Wow. I guess he really planned to take care of her if something happened. Poor bastard."

Josh nodded. "You think he was a bad husband?" he asked.

I thought about this. "I dunno. Probably not. I mean, not perfect, but who the hell is? She couldn't have been easy to live with, either. Takes two to tango."

"That's for sure."

We ate our lunches in silence for a few minutes, each lost in our own thoughts.

I thought about Belle and how I would have liked to dance a real tango with her. She once told me she loved to tango, but I had never followed up on it and now I had lost my chance. Story of my life. I guess I still wasn't over her, Dawn Coeur-Lyons notwithstanding.

I thought about Dawn and an oppressive sadness came over me. I wondered if she already realized that Jimmy wasn't going to take her away from her sordid life by The Bay. I wondered if she knew he was dead. I felt so bad for her, this woman I hardly knew and had met only once.

Then it dawned on me, pun intended, that she might have been arrested as part of the FBI operation. The prospect was so depressing and awful to think about that I didn't even ask Josh. Getting arrested after all she had been through, with such high hopes for her future. So sad. And my fault. Maybe I really was a boy zero after all.

My mind started wandering off in all sorts of strange directions. Maybe I could be the one to take her away from her sordid life by The Bay. Why not? She seemed to like me. I could offer her a better life, right?

No. Not really. I would just be rescuing another damsel in distress. Clearly, she appealed to some vulnerable part of my psyche. What about me wanted to rescue women like her? Crazy. I could never make a woman like Dawn happy.

"So whaddaya gonna do now?" asked Josh.

My reverie broken, momentarily fuddled, I stuttered. "Huh? Oh, I dunno. I got a call from the TransAmerica Life Insurance company."

Josh howled. "You're gonna sell life insurance?!"

"No!" I had to laugh at the prospect. "No, they were so impressed at how I had solved the case of Lamont Sloan—"

"And saved them a $10 million payout in the process."

"Yes, probably part of their motivation. Anyway, they were so impressed they offered me a job as an insurance fraud investigator. Can you believe it?"

"Well, you did solve the case and you did save them from having to pay out a helluva lot of money to Carmen."

"True. What about her, anyway?" I asked.

"You mean what's going to happen to her?"

"Yeah."

"Well, the coroner reached the same conclusion you did. No way could the two men have shot each other and then fired any additional shots. And, of course, only one bullet had been fired from each gun. Based upon our testimony that we heard two shots separated by several seconds, they determined that she must have fired the second one, the one that killed Sloan."

"So what happens to her?"

"The DA will probably go for life without parole. First-degree murder."

"You think he'll get it?" I wondered.

"I dunno. It's hard to make a premeditated homicide case, especially one like this, where she probably acted in the moment.

"And juries are funny, you know," he continued. "A beautiful woman facing destitution, a dead husband—and god knows what kind of fiction she'll make up to make it look like he was a horrible husband and abusing her and all that other crap that desperate people do. Any of those things might buy her a lesser charge. I suppose it also depends on how many women there are on the jury," Josh said. Then he laughed. "But seriously, what are you going to do now? I'll bet that after your success, any of the big detective agencies, like Pinkerton's, would hire you on and probably give you a salaried position with benefits and everything."

"Maybe." I shrugged. "I'm not sure I want to do this kind of work anymore. Yes, I could make good money at it. But I don't think I want to go back to that lifestyle. Too demanding and too, I guess, unsatisfying. I just didn't like it that much. I guess I'm just burned out. As for insurance, *hmmm*. Too smarmy."

Josh nodded in agreement.

"But there are other options," I said. "Did I tell you I got a letter from the Medical Board telling me they're going to reinstate my license in a few months?"

"No, you hadn't. That's great, though! So thinking of going back to medicine?"

"Medicine. Yeah, I could do that."

"Well, you gotta eat. If not that, what are you going to do for a living? I mean, you don't have some big retirement account hidden away, do you?"

"Oh, no," I shook my head. "Wish I did. No, I was thinking of something like, oh, I dunno, working with developmentally delayed kids or something like that. You know, something that has some meaning for me?"

"You're kidding," Josh said.

"No. Why?" I asked, puzzled.

He remained silent for a moment, slurping at his soda. "Digger, I just can't see you doing that. I think you'd get bored."

I thought about this and sighed. "You're probably right. I do have a little money. Turns out the Dutch company that owned the uncut diamonds put out a reward for their recovery. They've told me they're going to give me 250,000 Euros, whatever that translates to."

Josh whistled. "Wow! Not too shabby. About $300,000, I'm guessing. Maybe $200,000 after taxes. That's a good chunk o' change. I mean, you can't live on it, but you could take a break, take a vacation, you know, something like that."

"Are you thinking San Francisco again?"

"Ha ha! No, not that! You kill me, Digger."

I laughed too. Still, visiting Dawn again might be nice. Even if I was a boy zero. Maybe she would like to take a vacation with me.

I deliberately scuttled the idea as too stupid for words. "No, I was thinking more like the Bahamas or maybe the Caribbean."

"The Bahamas are in the Caribbean, Digger."

"Really? I guess I don't know the geography down there that well. Maybe I'll go to a travel agent and ask her to send me someplace warm where I can lie on a beach for a few weeks and read. That would be a nice break."

"Yeah, that does sound nice."

My mind traveled in a hazy sort of way to a tropical beach with palm trees swaying in a soft breeze, the sound of the ocean lapping on the shore, and pretty girls in skimpy bikinis bringing me ginger ales. As an interesting aside, in my vision of paradise, Dawn was relaxing in the sand next to me wearing nothing at all, her olive skin glistening in the sun. Someone once said the only way to get rid of temptation was to yield to it.

I tried to think of a good travel agent.

Josh interrupted my thoughts. "Okay, but what are you going to do when you get back from this dream vacation?"

I pondered this. "Well, an old friend called up last week. He works as a prison shrink up on the Central Coast and lives on some beach up there. He said I can visit any time I want."

"Oh, yeah? He must work at IMT up in Thomasville. I used to go up there on transports and such. It's a beautiful area."

"Really? I've never been up there."

"Oh, yeah. It's really nice. Simco Beach, Vulcan Bay, Morgan's Cove. You should go up there for a few weeks, Digger. With the reward money, you're probably set for at least a few months, maybe even have enough left over for a down payment on a house. You could go check it out and then come back with a clear head and figure out what you want to do next. Heck, you could probably be a police doctor if you wanted to work with us!"

"Forensics? *Hmmm.* I've never liked that kind of work."

"Oh, well, you know, whatever. You don't have to decide now."

"Yeah. But that'd be a good way to get back into the swing of things."

Having finished our lunches, we sat a few moments in silence. Then, as if on cue, two attractive young women came up to where we were sitting and started talking with folks at the other tables.

We watched them and kicked each other under the table.

Finally, they worked their way around to us.

"Hi!" said a bubbly blonde, "We're from NOW, the National Organization for Women!"

"Yeah!" said the other, a petite Asian brunette. "And we're soliciting for members! Would you like to join?"

Josh and I looked at each other, puzzled.

"I thought only women joined the National Organization for Women," I said.

"Oh, no!" said the blonde. "NOW is not just for women!"

"Yeah!" said the brunette. "NOW women are open to men too!"

I looked at her, then at the blonde, and then at Josh.

And then I started to laugh. I laughed harder than I'd laughed in years.

It must have been contagious, because, at first, the women looked offended. Then they started laughing too. Then Josh started laughing. We were howling our heads off.

People at other tables turned to stare, but I just kept laughing and laughing and laughing. Passersby stared as well, but I just kept laughing.

And pretty soon, everyone else was laughing—the girls, Josh, and everyone within earshot.

I guess there is something about laughter that just sort of makes things okay, reassures us that our troubles don't amount to a hill of beans in this crazy world.

I tried to breathe and the intoxicating scent of juniper and sage enveloped me.

And then, because I was laughing so hard, I couldn't breathe . . . *but* it felt good.

THE END

ACKNOWLEDGEMENTS

NO BOOK IS the creation of one individual. So, thanks to Josh Owens for his immensely helpful early edits of the book, which is infinitely better for his efforts. Thanks also to Deb Froese for her subsequent careful review of the manuscript and excellent suggestions. Her input, too, greatly improved the book. And finally, many heartfelt thanks to Emma Elzinga for her beautiful and haunting cover and interior design. Any author would be proud to have his or her work displayed so elegantly. A big thank you to my friend George Velmer, who introduced me to my agent Cathy Nakos. She in turn pitched the book to Georgette Green at Indigo River Press who graciously accepted a manuscript from an unknown author. And finally Jeremy Herman, who performed a thorough and excellent proof-read of the manuscript. Thanks, as always, to VPK, without whom none of my writing would be possible. All errors, omissions, or inaccuracies are my own. As always, my appreciation to my parents, my sister Sarah, and my brothers, Mark and Joey for their constant support and encouragement.